Hold Firm

Biker Daddy Bodyguards

Book 1

Sue Brown

BIKER DADDY BODYGUARDS #1

All Rights Reserved

Blurb

"Am I here as his bodyguard, his fake boyfriend, or his Daddy?"

The minute Quinn lays eyes on the bratty boy hunched in the chair, spitting fire and ice at him, he knows why he's been chosen for this assignment. He doesn't want to take the job but the boy's life is in danger. Could Quinn turn him away?

Cade doesn't want a bodyguard at his back 24/7. He works hard and parties harder. But this man isn't the usual rent-a-suit. He's six foot five of solid muscle, hard eyes, and a voice which makes Cade want to beg for his attention.

To the world, Quinn is Cade's bodyguard. To their friends, Quinn is Cade's boyfriend. To the suspect, Quinn is Cade's Daddy...

Quinn can't help thinking this won't end well.

To my Writer Shenanigans crew, Z.A. Maxfield, LE Franks, Belinda McBride, and Morticia Knight, who have been cheerleaders, broad shoulders, and founts of wisdom. Thank you, ladies. Without you, Biker Daddy Bodyguards wouldn't have been devised, let alone finished.

To my editor, Julia Talbot. You rock!

To my betas, Cinders Osborne, Lorraine Kay, Mary Anne Ostroman, and Ann Marie James, thank you for all your time and input into making the story better.

And last, but never ever least, my lovely office pal, Clare London, who is always the best.

Chapter One

Quinn

The phone call was an unwelcome start to Quinn's day. He fumbled for his cell phone on the nightstand, knocking over an empty whiskey tumbler in the process, and clapped it to his ear.

"Yeah?"

The loud noise continued. He squinted at the phone and pressed connect.

"Yeah?"

"Quinn Ryder?"

Even half-asleep, he knew the voice was a stranger. "Yeah. Who are you?"

"My name is Liam Quick from QuickFire Securities in London. I have a job for you."

British. Male. Hard edge to his tone. In the business.

Dammit, Quinn had to focus.

"Who gave you my number?"

"CDR."

Quinn sat up and ran his hand through his short hair,

wincing as a strand got caught in a split nail. "Send me the details."

"You need to be at CDR at ten this morning. They have the intel."

Quinn pressed his lips together. "I don't work for CDR."

"You're working for me, not them. I need a bodyguard with a certain skill set. Your name came up."

Sure it had, and he knew exactly who from.

"If you're based in London why do you need me?"

"My client is in Seattle. He's used me before. He contacted me and asked for my help."

"Why not use CDR's usual security teams? I'm semi-retired."

Burned out more like. But that wasn't something he was going to discuss with a complete stranger.

"As I said, you have a skill set we need."

Quinn was on the point of refusing when Quick played his trump card.

"Josh Cooper says hi."

Quinn groaned and thumped back onto the pillows. "Tell him to fuck off."

Quick laughed in his ear. "Ten o'clock. Don't be late."

He disconnected the call, leaving Quinn staring up at the ceiling with a mouth full of cotton from too much whiskey the night before and the realization he had to move or he'd be late.

Quinn managed a succinct, "Fuck!" At thirty-nine he was too old for this shit.

A chirrup in his ear made him turn his head to look into the remaining amber eye of his tabby cat, Mogs. She'd lost the right eye in a fight with a fox. Quinn had thought he'd lose her, but she'd recovered from the injuries, a lot scarred and minus one eye, but with more attitude than ever.

"What do you think, Mogs? Take the job or don't take the job?"

Stupid question. Burned out or not, he needed to make rent this month. He'd have to take the job or he'd be a rent-a-mall-cop again.

"Fucking Josh Cooper."

Quinn rumbled on his old Hog into the underground parking lot for CDR in downtown Seattle at one minute to ten. If they wanted him that badly they could wait a few minutes. He parked next to a new Harley Sportster, wondering who in CDR could afford a sweet ride like that. It was a shame he didn't have time to give it the appreciation it deserved. He'd been drooling over the latest model in his bike magazines, but he hadn't had a chance to see one up close and personal. He gave it a last regretful look before he headed for the elevators.

He didn't recognize the woman at the reception desk who told him to take a seat on one of the leather couches. She wore a skin-tight dress and too much red lipstick, but her smile was nice and the coffee she brought him was strong enough to get even his brain firing on all cylinders. He scrolled through bikes for sale on his phone until a voice made him look up.

"Quinn."

A voice that had haunted his nightmares for years.

"Dominic. Good to see you," he lied. He rose and held out his hand to the red-haired man who ran CDR with an iron fist.

"You're late," Dominic Cook snapped.

"I am now," Quinn retorted. They'd made him wait. He didn't work for CDR. He didn't have to be polite.

Dominic inclined his head as if Quinn had a point.

"Why am I here?" Quinn demanded.

"It's complicated. Come with me."

He led Quinn to a conference room. Quinn had spent a lot of time here. Huge windows stretched along two sides and if he bothered to gaze out he'd see a spectacular view of the Seattle business district skyline. Quinn didn't bother.

Two men sat at the conference table, their backs to the window. One screamed attorney with his ten-thousand-dollar suit and five-hundred-dollar hairstyle. Quinn ignored him. He turned to look at the other.

Instantly Quinn knew who he was and why Quinn was the one who'd gotten the call. Cade Connolly, Seattle's newest pop sensation, was twenty-five, tops, with hair the color of night and huge eyes a deep blue. It was a striking combination alongside his Slavic cheekbones.

Connolly worked hard and played harder. Rumor had it that Connolly and his band, Daysance, were about to hit the big-time. Correction. They'd already hit the big-time. Now they were about to go stratospheric, thanks to their charismatic lead singer. Quinn was more a blues guy, but even he'd been known to hum along with Cade Connolly if the radio was on.

Connolly glared at him, fire and ice in a black-clad leather package. Quinn stared back coolly until Connolly dropped his gaze and looked away, his lips pressed tightly together.

"This is Quinn Ryder. Quinn, this is Cade Connolly and his attorney, James Standish III," Dominic said.

"This is ridiculous," Connolly snapped. "I don't need him."

Quinn sighed inwardly. One of those clients. The ones who denied they needed a bodyguard right up until they got their brains blown out by some crazy guy.

"Now, Cade, you know that's not true," Standish began.

Quinn ignored him and sat opposite Cade, holding his gaze. He could see the anger and humiliation pouring like waves from the younger man. Whatever was going on, Cade was hurt and embarrassed.

"Tell me," Quinn ordered.

Connolly glowered at him. "They think I'm being stalked."

"Are you?"

"Yes." The word sounded as if it was dragged out of him over broken glass.

"Is it a man or woman?" He'd met both over the years. They operated differently so it was important to know from the start.

"Man. He was...my boyfriend."

Dominic handed Quinn a folder. He flipped it open to see a thirtysomething bear staring back at him with one arm wrapped around a younger, more innocent version of the man sitting opposite him. Connolly looked barely legal in the photo although this had to be in the last two years. To anyone else this would be a cute moment between them. To Quinn it looked possessive, dominating. He's mine, the bear was saying to the world. Hands off.

Quinn read the couple of paragraphs. Eric Strada, thirty-seven, boyfriend for two years. Broke up three months ago. Alleged to have killed Connolly's cat on his way out. Nice. Quinn had zero tolerance for anyone who hurt innocent animals. He frowned as he stared at the picture. He knew Strada. They mixed in the same circles, but they'd only spoken maybe once or twice.

He read the list of incidents. It followed a familiar pattern.

- Social media abuse
- Threatening letters
- Contacting Connolly's family and friends, begging them to make Cade take him back.
- Assaulting Cade outside a nightclub

The list went on. Strada was a nasty piece of work. Quinn gritted his teeth. The fact he'd not heard that Strada was an abusive piece of crap meant something was seriously wrong.

"He was violent to Cade," the attorney said. "He—"

"No!" Connolly ground out harshly. "Ryder doesn't need to know."

"Yes, I do," Quinn said, holding Cade's gaze. "I need to know what he did to you."

"I can't," Cade wrapped his arms around himself, rocking backward and forward.

Geez, the man had done a number on the kid.

Quinn looked at Dominic and Standish. "Get out."

Standish looked shocked, then shook his head. "I can't leave my client."

"You're gonna pay me to look after your client, so you can leave him," Quinn pointed out. He glanced at Dominic who nodded.

"Let's leave them alone for a few minutes, Standish."

The attorney went reluctantly, Dominic closing the door on the protests.

In the silence of the room, Quinn waited for Cade to speak. He was prepared to wait all day if necessary.

When Cade looked up, his eyes wrecked with pain, Quinn spoke. "What did he do to you?"

"He raped me."

"Once?"

Cade slumped in his seat, hiding his face from Quinn. "No."

"Cade."

Cade, not Connolly. Quinn knew he was going to take the case. Knew he had to take it.

The boy didn't move, didn't look up.

"Cade, look at me."

Quinn put the full weight of his authority in his voice. He expected to be obeyed.

Slowly, Cade raised his head. Unshed tears brimmed in his eyes, but his cheeks were dry. He was holding onto his control by a thread.

Quinn nodded, showing he was pleased. "Strada wasn't your boyfriend, was he?"

Cade wrinkled his brow. "Yes, he was."

Quinn shook his head. "Maybe to the outside world. But you and I know better. He was your Daddy."

"Yes."

A single tear ran down the boy's cheek.

"And he abused you."

"Yes."

Quinn gave a satisfied nod. "Good boy."

"I'm not your boy," Cade burst out. "I'm not your boy. I'm not your boy. I don't... I won't do that again. I don't need a Daddy."

Poor boy. He probably had that mantra on repeat in his

head. Quinn couldn't remember the last time he'd seen a boy so much in need of a Daddy.

"So why pick me as your bodyguard?"

"I didn't," Cade said bitterly. "I need security for an event I'm going to. Liam said he knew just the guy, and James—Standish—set up the meeting. I thought I was getting a team of bodyguards from CDR."

"You still can. Suited and booted." He wasn't going to force his way into Cade's life. "CDR has teams who could work with you."

"I just want to be left alone."

The pain tore at Quinn. He wanted to take Cade in his arms and protect him from the world, but Cade wasn't his. What did they expect from him? He stood and walked to the door, flinging it open.

"Where're you going?" Cade asked.

"Nowhere. I just need information."

Quinn whistled to attract Dominic and Standish's attention. Dominic scowled at being summoned like a dog. Quinn ignored him and walked around the table to stand behind Cade who looked up at him.

"Don't you want to sit down?"

"No."

The two men came in. Dominic sat where Quinn had been. Standish went to sit next to his client, but Quinn shook his head and pointed to a seat next to Dominic. The lawyer looked as if he was going to protest, but Dominic said, "Sit down, Standish."

When Standish took his place, Quinn spoke. "Let's start again and cut the bullshit. Why do you want me to be Cade's bodyguard?"

"You know why," Dominic said over Standish's spluttering.

"Say it so there's no mistake."

"Cade is headlining the entertainment at the bike expo event. It's a big deal. He needs someone who can fit in."

Quinn shook his head. "You've got half a dozen guys who ride motorbikes. Jace or Padraig would do."

"He needs someone who looks like you," Dominic said.

"Why?"

He needed it spelled out, so they were all clear. People didn't call him if they just wanted a bodyguard.

Dominic huffed. "He needs a Daddy. Strada needs to know Cade is off the market."

Finally.

"You're making a point or baiting him?"

"Both."

"Am I there as his bodyguard, fake boyfriend, or Daddy?" Quinn felt Cade twitch and laid a hand on his shoulder to calm him.

"All of the above," Dominic said.

"I don't need a boyfriend, and I definitely don't need a Daddy."

Quinn squeezed Cade's shoulder again and he subsided. Cade took direction so well. It was such a shame he'd been abused by a true bastard.

Quinn knew Dominic didn't miss a trick. The man knew how to read body language and knew exactly why Quinn stood behind Cade.

Standish seemed less certain. "Cade, CDR think it's best you have someone who will fade into the background."

Cade tilted his head to stare at Quinn. "Fade?"

Quinn understood Cade's dubious tone. Normal bodyguards faded into the background. With his gruff features and wearing leather head to toe, Quinn would stick out like a sore thumb to anyone who didn't know Cade.

"How long is the assignment?" He directed his question at Dominic.

"Two weeks to cover this event. Cade is traveling to London at the end of the month. Quickfire Securities is taking over."

Quinn had to bite back the "No!" threatening to spill out. Cade was not his boy. He didn't want another boy. He was a bodyguard for two weeks. End of assignment. He made rent.

"We want to get Strada before Cade leaves Seattle."

Quinn nodded. He was merely there as bait. He didn't like the idea, but he understood. The last thing they wanted was Strada traveling to London and causing chaos over there. Two weeks to catch an abuser… If Quinn let him live.

Cade

Cade hated to be seen. This man saw him.

He didn't want to be in this tight-assed office. He'd had a full-blown screaming tantrum when his management team had insisted he needed a full-time bodyguard. If he'd screamed like that in front of Eric he'd have been put over his knee and spanked so hard he'd have found it difficult to sit down for a week, but they just soothed and placated him and still he found himself here. He didn't want to be soothed and placated. He needed to be told what to do and disciplined when he was naughty. Cade pressed his lips together. He missed Eric and that was all kinds of sick considering what Eric had done to him. Cade hated himself for needing his Daddy.

Cade resented the fact that he was being forced to have a bodyguard or a security team. More people invading his life. He just needed to get away from Seattle for a while, which was why they'd scheduled London. One more event here, then Cade could breathe for a few weeks. Strada avoided flying. He wouldn't follow Cade to London, which was why they'd booked it.

This place suffocated Cade. He wanted to run and hide away from this huge, granite-jawed man who seemed to swallow up the space. The second Quinn had stepped into the room, Cade knew he was a Daddy. He had that same presence Eric did. And that made him dangerous. Cade didn't need another Daddy. That part of his life was behind him. He'd been a boy, but his Daddy had abused him. No more boy. He'd locked that side of his life away and vowed to be in control of his life, a fucking adult. He was going to tell Dominic to get rid of Quinn and just find him a suit. Quinn was the wrong person to take care of him.

Then Quinn had sat down and ordered everyone out of the room, fixed his hard brown eyes on him and, like a kid confessing everything, *like a fucking boy*, Cade had spilled out the toxic hurt of what Eric had done to him, and Quinn had just accepted it calmly. No judgement in his eyes. Cade wanted to sit on Quinn's lap, bury his face in his neck and howl because he knew Quinn could take it and make it better.

But Quinn wasn't his Daddy, and he wasn't a boy. And no one could make it better.

Cade tuned out Standish, who worried incessantly about details Cade wasn't interested in. Dominic answered him with a patience borne of long experience. Quinn said nothing but he didn't take his hand off Cade's shoulder. It grounded him. Once, he started jiggling his leg and Quinn gently squeezed his shoulder until he stopped. And then Cade hated himself for giving in and obeying the unspoken order.

"I want to get Cade home," Quinn said, cutting through yet another discussion by Standish. The man was dear to Cade, but right now he would have gladly strangled him.

"Uh, yes," Standish said.

Quinn turned to Dominic. "Do you have a vehicle?"

Cade sat up straighter. "My Harley's in the parking lot."

"No," Quinn said flatly.

Cade did not just hear that. He tilted his head. "No?" he said icily. "What do you mean, 'no'?"

"You're not riding solo until I've thoroughly assessed the situation. Beyond this folder I have no idea how dangerous Strada is."

Cade wrenched away from Quinn's hold, leapt to his feet, and glared at him. "You're not stopping me riding my bike. You ride. You're supposed to ride with me."

"Not yet."

"This isn't what we agreed," Standish said.

Quinn folded his arms across his massive chest and stared them all down. Cade despised himself a little more for finding that dominance a turn-on. Of course Quinn was dominant; he was a Daddy. Cade could never let himself forget that.

"Quinn—" Dominic started.

"I'm taking Cade home in one of the SUVs. You have to get our bikes back somehow. Once I've assessed the danger, Cade will be able to resume riding if he has two escorts."

"No fucking way!" Cade was not a fucking prisoner.

"It's only in the short-term, Cade," Standish said, trying to be soothing. "You can't afford for anything to go wrong for this show. You're the main attraction. You've got a lot of money riding on this."

Cade glared at his attorney. He was right. Cade couldn't afford to fuck this up. The abuse Strada had been throwing his way had already made some of the show's investors edgy. They didn't want to be associated with bad publicity and there had been talk of replacing him. It had taken fast talking by his management team and threats of lawsuits from his attorney to get them to back off. They were the ones who'd insisted he had full-time security until the show was over. CDR was the best, and the only way he could afford to pay for it was to keep working.

"I've got my own car," he snapped finally.

To his surprise, Dominic nodded. "His driver is good. Trained by us."

"Okay, get him here," Quinn said, once again giving the orders. "We need to get moving."

Cade curled his lip as his thousand-dollar-an-hour attorney jumped to the orders of a low-level muscle-man and made the call.

"Cade."

He turned to look at Dominic. "Yeah?"

"I know this is scary but believe me, this is our job, and Quinn is one of the best. By the time you go to London we'll have this resolved."

"I'm not scared," he insisted.

"It's okay to admit you are. It doesn't make you weak."

Cade shook his head. "I lived with him. Then I was scared. Now I'm angry that he won't stay the hell out of my life."

"I understand," Quinn rumbled, "but the fact he won't stay away needs to be handled. Once guys like him get an obsession they don't back down."

"Guys like you?" Cade challenged.

"Cade!" Standish spluttered, but Quinn held up his hand and the lawyer subsided.

"Some dominants without a focus or control can be

obsessive, yes. Not all. I'm lucky, my work keeps me focused."

Right now, that laser focus on Cade was too much to handle.

"Eric doesn't need to work. He's got a trust fund."

Quinn didn't sneer at the information like a lot of people did, but neither did he look impressed. Cade filed that piece of information away. Was he impressed by wealth or had he seen so much of it in his work it was irrelevant?

"Strada has a focus and that's you," Quinn said. "We use that to draw him in."

"You're making me the bait?" Cade didn't like that idea.

"I don't want Cade in danger," Standish said.

Cade reached over and patted Standish's hand. His attorney was like a father figure to him.

"He won't be," Quinn assured him. "I'm going to be the bait, not Cade. Strada will want to get me out of the picture."

"So you'll pose as my boyfriend, and he'll go after you?" Cade wasn't sure he liked that idea any better. The thought of the vibrant man opposite him being injured or worse made him want to hurl.

"We'll talk about it later," Quinn assured him.

Cade nodded uncertainly. He wrapped his arms around himself, needing the reassurance of a hug even if it was just from himself. He jumped when Quinn laid a hand on his shoulder and fixed him with a steady gaze.

"It'll be okay, Cade, I promise."

Cade wanted to ask Quinn to hold him. If Quinn had been his real Daddy, Cade would have begged him to wrap his muscular arms around him and ground him. He needed it so much. Eric hadn't comforted him. He'd held him down and hurt him. A sob erupted from his throat before he could stop it.

He wrenched away from Quinn before he did something stupid like beg for his embrace. Quinn frowned, but he stepped back and gave Cade some space. Cade forced air into his lungs. "I need to get out of here," he muttered.

"Your car is here," Dominic said. "It's in the underground parking lot. I'll arrange for your bikes to be delivered later today."

There was nothing Cade wanted more than to run to his Hog and ride away from Standish, and Dominic, and the thought of Strada, but mostly he wanted to run away from Quinn Ryder who was making him want things he'd put behind him.

Chapter Two

Quinn

Cade protested the entire ride home. CDR had promised to deliver their motorbikes to Cade's house. Cade didn't like it. Quinn didn't care. He wasn't letting Cade on his bike until he'd set ground rules.

Quinn let Standish do the talking, who was returning to see his client settled, and then he was going home. He saw no point getting involved as, whether Cade liked it or not, he had a bodyguard. He sat next to the chauffeur and ignored the heated argument in the back while he read the information on Eric Strada again. Quinn had met the man briefly when he traveled to San Francisco. This must have been before Eric was involved with Cade. Quinn had received no negative vibes from the man, but he hadn't spoken to him long enough or formed a friendship with him, to make a sound judgement. He had a phone call to make as soon as he had free time. If Eric Strada wasn't caught and he gave up his obsession with Cade, he'd be looking for another boy. Cade couldn't have been the only one he abused.

Quinn needed to do some more digging and not through CDR. The Daddy world was small enough that he knew who to speak to.

Cade's voice rose and Quinn caught the chauffeur rolling his eyes.

"Is he always this noisy?" Quinn asked, his voice low.

The driver didn't answer but the silence was enough for Quinn. Cade was a brat. One hundred percent brat. But a boy who had been abused too. Quinn had his own methods for dealing with bratty boys, but he also knew how to tread lightly when the situation needed.

"What's your name?"

"Long. Gareth Long." Gareth had a Welsh burr to his accent.

"Okay if I call you Gareth?"

The driver shrugged. "Call me what you like. And you?"

"Quinn Ryder. Security."

"You'll have your hands full there, Quinn." Gareth kept his voice down low but with Cade's incessant ranting there wasn't much chance of being heard.

"Yeah, I see that. I'll put a stop to that when we get back to his place. I'm not spending two weeks listening to him shout."

"Good luck with that one."

He heard the doubt in Gareth's voice. But Quinn was an experienced bodyguard and an experienced Daddy, and he was not letting Cade get away with pushing him around for two weeks.

"How long have you been working for Mr. Connolly?"

"I work for the record company now. They sponsored my employment visa. But I used to work for Cade in the UK whenever he visited. He got to like me. Then he found out I was looking for a change in scene and suggested I come to the States and he would give me somewhere to live. There's an apartment above the garage. I drive him occasionally and take care of the maintenance, and spend the rest of my time working for the record company. He's good, despite the noise. Better than most employers I've worked for. And when the time is right, I've got a plane ticket home."

Quinn was impressed. He wouldn't have thought Cade would have given a crap about his employees.

"I was the one who took him to hospital," Gareth said quietly. "And I was the one who suggested he call Liam Quick. I've worked with Liam before."

"So you knew Strada was beating him up?" Quinn's voice was equally low, but the judgement was in his tone.

Gareth pressed his lips together. "I knew there were issues, but Cade told me to butt out. He made it clear my interference wasn't welcome. I kept my mouth shut until the last time, and then I told him I was calling the authorities whether he liked it or not. He begged me not to call the police, and I agreed if I could call Liam."

Quinn understood Cade not wanting the police involved, even if he didn't agree with the decision. It would become a media shit show and Cade would be the target, not Strada. "You did the right thing."

"Did I?" Gareth sounded bitter. "I said nothing as a nasty piece of work beat up my employer."

"You did what I asked," Cade said. He'd obviously overheard the conversation and he leaned forward to squeeze Gareth's shoulder, in what seemed like a very comforting gesture.

Then he turned an angry gaze on Quinn. "I don't appreciate you interrogating my employees."

Quinn raised an eyebrow and Cade looked away. "I

need to find out everything to keep you safe." He raised the file. "This tells me nothing beyond the basics, which means you're hiding things. And secrets will get you killed. If you're not prepared to talk to me, then I will talk to everyone else. If Gareth knew Strada was being abusive, other people will too."

"Now that's going a bit too far," Standish protested.

Quinn turned to look at him. "You knew and you didn't make an effort to stop it. You could have called the police any time."

Standish went beet red, and Quinn expected an angry outburst, but he merely looked away, saying, "I tried. I tried."

Which meant Cade had put the muzzle on him too. Quinn was going to get to the bottom of this, but not now, not in the car while they all sat in angry silence.

* * *

When they arrived at Cade's large house on Capitol Hill, Quinn told everyone to stay in the car while he liaised with one of CDR's teams. He knew the three men who greeted him at the gate.

"The place is clear. We've been through it from top to bottom. Didn't expect to see you back at CDR," Doug said with a smirk.

"I didn't expect it either," Quinn admitted ruefully.

"The boss says we are to stay out of your way unless there's a problem. As far as everyone is concerned, you're the boyfriend not the bodyguard. The only people who know what's going on are the three teams and Dominic. We'll liaise with you and only you."

"Good. Unless Strada manages to take me out of the

picture, don't liaise with the client. He doesn't seem to have the best judgement."

Doug tilted his head. "So you're going to be the bait."

Quinn grimaced. "It seems so. It's not the first time. But first I need to organize my cat."

Doug laughed. "Have you still got old Mogs? She must be what – fourteen?"

Mogs was the one thing guaranteed to make Quinn smile. He adored his cat and most of the security men he met fell in love with her too. She was scruffy and high maintenance, but he loved her.

"You've got a cat?"

Quinn exchanged a resigned look with Doug, and turned to see Cade standing behind him, a strangely hopeful look on his face. "You're supposed to be in the car."

"I got bored," Cade said petulantly. "What are you going to do with your cat while you're away?"

"The same thing I always do," Quinn said as he guided Cade into the house. "I'll ask my neighbor to look after her. Mogs is fourteen years old and spends most of the time asleep. She's no bother to anyone. Stay here." He made it an order, ignoring the immediate scowl on Cade's face.

He jogged to the car where Standish still sat in the back. "Go home," he said. "Leave Cade with me."

The relief was obvious on the attorney's face, but he said, "I ought to make sure he's settled."

"Go home," Quinn insisted. "Get some rest. Let me do my job."

"You can call me if—"

Quinn shut the car door and banged the top. Gareth pulled away.

One issue dealt with, now he had to deal with the other one.

Cade wasn't where Quinn had left him. He was nowhere to be seen. Quinn growled under his breath. Bratty boys deserved to have their asses reddened if they misbehaved.

He found Cade in the kitchen. Or, more to the point, he found Cade headfirst hunting through one of the kitchen cabinets. The sight of his butt poking out was almost more than Quinn could bear.

"Lord, I can only deal with so much temptation."

Cade backed out from the cabinet, his face red and hair muzzed as he emerged holding a small bowl.

"You could bring Mogs here," he said, holding up the bowl with a triumphant smile. "She's welcome and I have cat bowls and a litter tray. I still have scratching posts in nearly every room. My cat was a menace and scratched everywhere." Quinn didn't move and Cade's expression dropped. He seemed to close in on himself. "Or not. Whatever." He dropped the bowl with a clatter on the countertop and went to walk past Quinn.

Dammit, he'd upset Cade. Quinn got in Cade's path and smiled at him. "It's kind of you to offer, Cade. I'm not sure you'd want her here though. She's scarred from too many fights, and very grumpy. She's not this sweet and adorable cat who likes being hugged."

Cade laughed and the tense lines of his shoulders eased a fraction. "You should have met Charlie. He was all teeth and claws. The only person he liked was me. I think that was one of the reasons Eric killed him. Charlie really hated Eric."

Quinn warmed to Cade's deceased cat. Obviously, he'd had better sense than the humans in Cade's life. "If you're sure. I'll get Mogs and bring her here later today."

"Can't I go with you? I'd like to see where you live."

"We'll see," Quinn said without making a firm commitment. As far as he was concerned, Cade was on house arrest unless he was working.

Cade shot him a suspicious look, but he nodded. "Do you want to look around the house?"

"Yeah, why don't you show me?"

"You know I'm the client, right? I tell you what to do."

Quinn leaned into Cade's space, until Cade was almost bending backward. He took it slowly, careful not to scare the boy. Then he heard the hitch in Cade's breath, saw the almost comically wide eyes. Quinn glanced down. No, Cade wasn't scared. He was turned on. Quinn's dick hardened at the sight and scent of this boy. He had to put a stop to that idea right away. He was protecting Cade from danger, that was all.

"No," Quinn said firmly.

Cade's brows furrowed together. "No?"

"No. You are the client, but it's my job to keep you alive. Which means when I tell you to stay somewhere, you stay there."

"You're just the bait," Cade taunted him.

"I'm the bait, the hook, the line, and the man who's gonna sink Strada," Quinn said.

"You're very full of yourself," Cade said, although Quinn was very sure he wasn't aware how breathy his voice was.

"That's my job. Forget the idea of me fading into the background, boy, I'm front and center."

Cade's expression changed, and he was the one to take a step back. "I'm not your boy. You're my bodyguard, not my Daddy."

"As far as Strada is concerned, I'm your new Daddy and you are going to have to act like it." Quinn fixed his gaze on

Cade who seemed to want to look anywhere except at him. "I need your cooperation, Cade, or this won't work, and I may as well walk out the door now."

"I don't know," Cade said, his voice shaky, and he wrapped his arms around himself.

Quinn wasn't bothered by Cade's lack of confidence. This was a new job and they had to get to know each other. The only person Cade knew was Liam, and he wasn't here. It was up to Quinn to instill confidence in his boy—his fake boy.

"You leave me to do my job. You obey my orders when I give them, and in return I let you do your job. It's two weeks until you leave for London. Do you think you can work with me until then?"

"Work *with* you. The operative word is *with*," Cade said sourly.

Quinn chuckled. "It's a give-and-take, Cade. We play happy Daddy and boy in public and you get to ride on your sweet bike and get freedom to do your job."

Cade looked up at him, his face pinched. "I don't want another Daddy. I don't need another Daddy."

Oh poor boy. He desperately needed a Daddy. A real one. It was just a shame it wasn't going to be Quinn.

Cade

Cade couldn't hide the hurt in his voice. He wanted to huff and shout and rail against Quinn's rules. When he went to DEFCON Brat it was easier to forget his longing for another Daddy. He especially hated the way his body relaxed at Quinn's calm voice for the first time since his management team had given him the ultimatum. He would not roll over and obey just because a Daddy gave him orders.

Adult. His world. His rules.

"What are your plans for today?" Quinn asked.

"I cleared my schedule because Standish asked me to. Tomorrow I've got a seven am session in my studio. My band will be coming here."

"What are their names?" Quinn asked.

Cade listed the names.

"I'll send them to the team on the gate," Quinn said. "That way they don't get refused entry tomorrow morning."

"You know they're not Eric, yeah?" Cade commented dryly. "We know who the bad guy is."

"No one gets close to you unless I say so," Quinn said implacably.

Cade noticed he didn't agree or disagree with him about the band being good guys. "I need them, to do my job."

"We'll run background checks on them this afternoon."

"Do you always have to have the last word?"

"Yes," Quinn said with a deadpan expression, then he winked, and the frustration in Cade's mind eased a fraction.

"Why don't you take me around your home and then we'll sit and make a plan." Quinn made it sound like a suggestion, not an order, and Cade had nothing better to do.

As they wandered upstairs, Quinn asked, "Did you have a designer to decorate your home?"

Cade shook his head. "I did it myself."

"You did?"

Cade bristled at the skeptical note in Quinn's voice.

"This is the first place I've ever had to call my own. I grew up in the foster care system. I never stayed in a home for long."

"You were never adopted?" Quinn asked.

Cade didn't need Quinn's misplaced pity. "It didn't matter. I wasn't hurt or abused or anything like that. I just never stayed anywhere for very long. They found me hard work." He pulled a face. "I *was* hard work. It's only recently I was diagnosed with ADHD. That's why I bounce off the walls. But on the plus side, it helps with my creativity." He pointed to a painting on the wall. "That's one of mine. I couldn't decide what I wanted to be. So I do everything. It's just the music is making me money at the moment."

Quinn stared at the painting and then at Cade. "I've followed your art for years. I didn't put you and ConC together. Wow."

Cade was taken aback by the awe in his expression. "You're into street art?"

"I'm into all art, although I can't draw to save my life. But I follow a lot of young artists. I prefer street art to old Masters. I think your style is the most original I've ever seen."

Cade was touched to see the big man blush. Cade had never really decided what he wanted to focus on. Before the music contract, he'd gotten an international reputation as an up-and-coming artist, thanks to a breakout piece of art on an old wall in downtown Seattle. He loved his art, he loved his music. He wanted to do both, but the music sucked up all his time.

Cade slipped off his jacket to hang up in his bedroom, but he took a step back when Quinn leaned forward to study the ink on his arms.

"Sorry." Quinn smiled at him. "I didn't mean to startle you. Is that your work?"

"Some," Cade said, glancing at it indifferently. "I go to different artists to do the ink. I like their work. You like tattoos?"

"I always have." Quinn took off his own jacket and pushed up the sleeves of his sweater to reveal full sleeves of work.

"Nice!" Cade leaned forward to study Quinn's arms. "That's Jack Booker, isn't it?"

"You recognize his work?"

Cade nodded. "I study all the tattoo artists."

"He's my brother-in-law," Quinn admitted. "I was one of his first guinea pigs." He pulled a wry face. "He's gotten better since the early days."

"Booker is your brother-in-law?." Now it was Cade's turn to be awed. "Amazing. I can't wait to meet him. Can I meet him?"

"Sure." Quinn chuckled. "But he's not that exciting."

"He is to me," Cade said. "He's one of the reasons I started painting."

"You never thought of being a tattoo artist yourself?" Quinn asked.

Cade shook his head. "I never wanted to ink people. I faint at the sight of too much blood."

Quinn burst out laughing, and Cade scowled.

"I'm not kidding. When I get my own work done, I can't look at it until they've wiped away all the blood."

"There we have something in common," Quinn admitted. "I can deal with patching up wounds and injuries in the field, but if one of my nieces even has a graze on her knee or I'm bleeding myself, I wanna hurl."

The doorbell rang and to Cade's amusement, Quinn jumped back, his eyes wide. "What the hell?"

Cade grinned. "Yeah. Good, isn't it? The previous owner installed it. He was hard of hearing."

"Good is not the word I'd use. Deafening maybe,"

Quinn muttered as he went to answer the door. He looked back at Cade. "Get out of sight," he ordered.

Cade glowered at the abrupt order, but he obeyed, heading into the kitchen. He couldn't resist hovering by the doorway. Quinn strode over to the door and peered through the peephole.

Quinn turned, frowning when he saw Cade, but he said, "It's UPS. Are you expecting anything to be delivered?"

"Not today," Cade said.

"Okay." Quinn turned back to the door. "Who is it?"

"UPS. Delivery for Mr. Connolly."

Cade relaxed, recognizing the delivery man's voice.

"Show me your ID through the peephole. Leave the box on the door."

"You've gotta sign for it."

Quinn flung the door open and Cade spotted a stocky kid standing on the step with a long box, the kind for delivering long stemmed flowers.

He emerged from the kitchen, but Quinn waved at him and he retreated back to the doorway.

"Oh, hey, Cade." The kid waved at him.

"Hi, Juan," Cade said. "How's your mom?"

"She's good. The baby's due soon."

Quinn took delivery of the box. The kid seemed unfazed by Quinn's caution and once he'd gotten his signature, he said goodbye to Cade, and clattered back down the steps toward his truck. Quinn shut the door and looked at Cade.

"You know him?"

"Yeah. He's harmless. His mom's a fan."

Cade held his hand out for the box, but Quinn shook his

head. "It's from a florist." He read out the address and Cade pulled a face. "It's from Batty Brenda."

"Who?"

"A fan of mine. Her online name is Tessie235. I call her Batty Brenda because she reminds me of an old neighbor. She is irritating, not dangerous, and apart from the flowers and the letters, she's never tried to hurt me or contact me. I give the flowers to my assistant. She really likes them."

"How long has she been doing this for? How many fans do you have who know where you live?"

Cade shrugged. He just accepted it as a cost of being part of the band. "I don't know. My management company deals with the letters, but I can't avoid the flowers being sent here. I just tell them another bouquet has arrived and they make a note."

"I'm going to put a stop to that. Tessie235 needs to save her money and quit stalking you." Quinn snapped a picture of the florist's name, then he opened the box without asking Cade if it was okay.

"You do know the flowers were sent to me," Cade pointed out.

Quinn grunted. "Does she normally send you black roses?"

Cade blinked. "No, that's different. She usually sends me carnations because I once said that I liked red carnations."

"I don't think these are from Tessie 235. I think these are from your former Daddy." He tilted the box to show Cade.

The roses were beautiful in an 'I long for your death' kind of way.

"If I were into goth, I would be thrilled to receive these," Cade said coming over to study the flowers.

"Is there any connection between Strada and black roses?"

Cade shook his head. "Not that I know of. Is there a note?"

Quinn opened a small envelope and his expression turned grim. "I don't think these are from Tessie."

"What does it say?" Cade demanded. When Quinn hesitated, he said, "You can't hide this from me. I'm an adult, Quinn, even if I like to be a boy. You have to tell me."

Quinn read from the small card.

You will always be mine

"Succinct," Cade said, aiming for flippant, but he knew his voice shook.

"What do you want me to do with the flowers?" Quinn said.

"I'm not giving these to Maria. Throw them in the trash," Cade muttered.

Quinn did as Cade asked, but he slipped the small card into his pocket. "I need to talk to the security team."

"Why?"

"I want to know why the delivery guy passed them so easily," Quinn explained. "He shouldn't have been able to approach the front door."

"I can answer that one. There's a gate around the side. Fans come to the front, so delivery drivers know to go to the side gate."

Quinn's expression darkened. "Does Strada know about this entrance?"

"Yeah. I mean he lived here too."

"Does he have a key?"

Cade shook his head. Changing the locks had been one of the first things he did when he threw Eric out of his life. "Not now, and all the keys and codes were changed to the house. That kid's a regular so he got the new code."

"The codes need to be changed again. No one gets past the team."

Cade sighed and scrubbed a hand through his hair. "I feel like I'm a prisoner."

"It's for two weeks. That's all," Quinn assured him.

"What if you don't catch him?"

"I'll catch him," Quinn said.

"You promise?"

Quinn's eyes softened a fraction. "Cade, I promise."

Chapter Three

Quinn

Quinn didn't give his promises lightly. He stepped into Cade's space again and rested his hands on Cade's shoulders, making each movement slow to give Cade a chance to back away if he wanted. Cade's shoulders shook but he stayed where he was and Quinn gave a brief squeeze before taking a step back. "I'm here, and I'm not going to let anyone hurt you. I'm sticking by your side until it really pisses you off, but we'll find Strada and then I will gut him."

"Did you mean arrest him?" Cade asked, one winged eyebrow raised.

"No."

Cade bit his lip, but he didn't argue.

"Do you want to show me where I'm sleeping tonight?" Quinn asked, trying to give the boy something else to think about. He could talk to the security team in a few minutes.

Cade nodded, but the tension didn't ease from his expression.

"Hey, Cade."

Cade seemed to come back to life. "Okay. Let me show you upstairs and then perhaps we could see about getting your cat? And when are our bikes due to be delivered from CDR?"

"All good questions. One thing at a time."

"You're not stopping me riding my bike," Cade warned.

Quinn didn't argue. Cade was going to find out about the limits of his activities soon enough. Why provoke an argument now?

* * *

The master bedroom was a study in blues and browns. It was stylish and classy, and not what he expected from the young man.

Cade snorted when Quinn looked at him in surprise. "What did you expect? Guitars on the walls and bike posters? Or my art?"

"Either. Both."

"At least you're honest." Cade seemed to fold in on himself, wrapping his arms around his body, comforting himself. "Eric never liked the guitars and posters. He banned them from the bedroom. He said they were too distracting. And he hated my paintings."

"You could have put them back up," Quinn suggested.

"Yeah, but maybe he was right. I like chilling out before I sleep, otherwise I'm thinking about art and music and bikes all night." He looked a little sheepish. "I hate the fact he was right about something."

"I understand."

"You do?" Cade looked surprised.

"The man physically abused you. It doesn't mean to say

he got everything wrong. You're the bigger man for accepting there were some things he got right."

"I wish he would go away, just fuck off, you know?"

Quinn wanted to hold Cade and take away his pain, but he couldn't. He had to stay professional. "That's what we're here for. To get you away from him."

Cade ran his hand through his hair and emitted the longest, most painful sigh Quinn had ever heard. "I know. But it's me who has to live under lockdown, not him."

"It's a short-term issue while we work out a long-term solution, Cade."

Cade gave him a wry smile. "In other words, put up and shut up."

"Yeah." Quinn was pleased Cade could retain some degree of humor. "Cooperate with us, and we'll get Strada out of your life."

"Let me show you your room."

Cade led the way out of the bedroom. Quinn didn't miss the fact that he'd not given his assent. Any cooperation he got from Cade would be hard-won. He didn't push it now. Later he would probably wish he'd been more forceful in extracting a promise from his client.

The guest bedroom was pleasant enough. Quinn paid little attention to his surroundings. It was just somewhere to bunk. He had more important things to worry about. He dumped his bag by the bed and looked at Cade who stood in the doorway.

"Okay. Next on the list I need to get Mogs."

"Your cat?" Cade's eyes lit up at Quinn's nod. "Can I come with you?"

"Yeah." After the delivery of the roses, Quinn wasn't leaving him alone, and if taking him to pick up his cat secured long-term cooperation, that worked for him. "Is Gareth still available?"

"He drives me whenever I want." Cade grimaced. "I prefer my bike, but they still insist Gareth follows me. Do you know what that does for my reputation?" His unimpressed expression spoke volumes.

Quinn could imagine. He held back a grin. "They just want to keep you safe."

"I know," Cade said dismissively. "Let's get your cat."

Quinn frowned as Cade stalked downstairs. He was the one who gave the orders. Cade was going to have to learn this fast.

By the time he reached the bottom of the stairs, Cade had his jacket slung over his shoulder and the front door open.

Quinn took a deep breath and counted to ten. He pushed the front door shut and stared down at Cade. "Did you check if Strada was outside before you opened the door?"

Cade pressed his lips together. "I'm not an idiot."

Not an answer.

"From now on, you don't answer the door first or go out without me checking it's safe," Quinn said. "I need to advise the team we're leaving so they can arrange an escort."

"Why don't you just handcuff me while you're at it?" Cade spat.

"If you don't obey my rules, it might come to that."

Two things happened. One, Cade's breath hitched. Was it at the mention of handcuffs or rules? He didn't manage to hide his excitement. Two, he narrowed his eyes at Quinn.

"I'm not your prisoner."

"You said you're not stupid. Then prove it."

"How?" Cade demanded.

Quinn held back from rolling his eyes with an effort. "You've had a security detail before, and you know the routine. I'm here to protect you."

"Then protect me by getting us out of here," Cade growled.

If Quinn thought Cade was going to cooperate easily, he was mistaken. Cade was going to fight him all the way. Quinn sighed. He called the security team. "We're leaving in five."

"Ready," Padraig said.

Quinn disconnected the call and peered through the window by the side of the front door.

"Okay, it's clear. Gareth is outside waiting. You stay behind me, head straight for the car and get in."

Cade huffed, but he did as he was told. Quinn waited until he was in, then he turned to Doug. "Change all the codes to the house and make sure the side gate is secure. We had a delivery guy turn up."

"We knew he was there. Ronan spotted him. He was vetted before he got to the door."

Quinn breathed easier. "Next time warn me."

"We tried," Doug pointed out, an edge to his tone.

Quinn checked his phone. Missed Call. "Dammit. I'm sorry."

"He wouldn't have gotten to the house if we didn't vet him first."

"Thanks, Doug."

"No worries."

Cade raised an eyebrow at Quinn as he slipped into the car beside him. "The hired help doesn't usually sit next to the client."

"He does in this case."

Quinn waited for Cade to challenge him, but the boy

just huffed again and stared out of the window. So they were going to sit in stony silence. The car pulled away, Padraig following behind them on his bike. Silence was fine with Quinn, and he spent the uneventful journey making a list of people to talk to when he got back.

He lived in a small apartment which was practical rather than aesthetic, but Cade didn't seem to care, more interested in the grumbly cat weaving around his feet. Mogs ignored Quinn in favor of the boy who sat on the floor-boards to love on her. Cade had bowls, so Quinn collected her favorite toys and food, plus her bed which she'd never slept in, and more clothes for himself. He stuffed a couple of thrillers in the bag too and his Switch. If he was on duty, he didn't get much time to play but it was good to wind down occasionally.

Mogs was in heaven, nestled in Cade's lap, and for the first time, Quinn saw true happiness in his smile and his soft expression. When they got through this, he would find some way of giving Cade a cat of his own. Briefly, he wondered about the wisdom of bringing his cat where Strada could potentially get at her, then Cade looked up and Quinn didn't have the heart to change their plans. The little monster even went in the travel cage without the fuss she usually made.

"You take Mogs. I'll take the bags. Don't go out until I've checked the area," he warned.

Cade didn't argue, just crooned at Mogs, who purred in return. Quinn wondered if he should do all his negotiations when Cade was holding a cat. It certainly dialed down the brattiness—and the noise.

For the journey back, Quinn sat next to Gareth who grinned at him. "You know you're never going to get your cat back."

"It might be worth it for a quiet life," Quinn muttered.

"I'm not deaf," Cade said.

Quinn was so tempted to respond to that, but his phone rang. His heart sank when he saw it was Padraig.

"Yes."

"We've picked up a tail. A Nissan Rogue."

"Okay. We'll divert. Keep me posted."

Gareth gave him a brief glance. "Problems?"

"Maybe. A tail. A Nissan Rogue. Take the long way home."

"On it. I don't know anyone who drives a Nissan. Strada prefers his Harley to a car."

"Good to know. Do you get other tails?"

"Yes. Obsessed fans, occasional paparazzi, even musicians trying to work with Cade."

"What's your usual MO?"

"I get Cade the hell away from the tail."

Quinn nodded approvingly at Gareth's declaration. "Do it without killing him or my cat."

He turned to look at Cade who just seemed resigned. "It happens all the time."

"We'll make a list of stalkers," Quinn said.

"They're just part of my life. I don't even notice them anymore."

Quinn grunted. Noticing was his job. He pulled down the visor to look in the mirror. Padraig was shadowing them, the Nissan behind the bike. He watched as Gareth took a few corners. The Nissan followed him every time.

"Drive to CDR. I don't want them following us home."

"On it," Gareth said.

Quinn relayed this information to Padraig, knowing he would organize their entrance to CDR.

The Nissan stayed with them, almost on top of

Padraig's motorbike at times. Quinn was frustrated, unable to see who was in the car. From Cade and Padraig's lack of reaction he had almost ruled out Strada, but he wasn't going to discount anything until he looked at Padraig's cameras.

Gareth slowed and turned into CDR's underground parking lot, Padraig following him. Quinn turned to look out the back window, noticing Cade was still focused on Mogs. The Nissan slowed, then drove on. Padraig had turned the bike and was obviously waiting to see if the Nissan would return.

They sat for a few minutes. When Padraig gave them the thumbs up, Quinn let out an explosive breath. "If there's any trouble, get the hell out of here," he said to Gareth.

"On it."

He turned to Cade. "Don't get out of the car."

"Sure," Cade agreed, still loving on Mogs who was sound asleep in the cage.

He was so calm, Quinn wondered if Strada had killed Cade's cat knowing it was one of the things that would calm him down. Did he want to leave Cade permanently on edge?

Quinn strode over to the bike, which Padraig had left idling. "Sitrep."

"It's gone. CCTV has tracked it down the street and right at the intersection. It didn't stop. The feed from my camera is already with the tech guys. From what I saw, it was a late middle-aged woman."

"Batty Brenda?"

Quinn had made sure they all knew about Cade's girl-friend on the ride over.

"Maybe, although I thought her MO was hearts and flowers, not stalking him."

"She could be escalating," Quinn pointed out.

"That means we're dealing with two stalkers."

"The driver says this isn't uncommon."

"Cade is famous," Padraig agreed.

"We need to identify the occupant from the Nissan and anyone else with a hard-on for Cade."

Quinn was profoundly uneasy at the idea of anyone and everyone following Cade. Gareth was obviously trained to a degree but it still left Cade vulnerable. If they followed him home, that meant a whole lot of bad guys knew where he lived.

"Okay, let's get home," Quinn said, "before my cat pisses in the car."

He jogged back to the car and slid in. "The Nissan is gone. We're going home."

"Any idea who it is?" Gareth murmured.

"It was a woman, not Strada," Quinn said.

"Fan, then."

"Maybe." Quinn had seen psychos recruit women before to stalk their victim and get a better idea of their movements. Cade might be more relaxed at the idea of a woman following him because he'd think they were less dangerous. In Quinn's experience, female perps were different, not less dangerous.

Gareth drove out of the parking lot, Padraig behind them. Despite them being extra cautious they saw no sign of the Nissan or other tails and they arrived back at Cade's house without incident.

Cade took Mogs into the house, leaving Quinn to bring in the bags.

"You do remember she's old and grumpy, don't you?" Quinn asked, when Cade showed no sign of putting her down.

The old and grumpy cat kneaded Cade's thighs with her paws and settled back down to sleep, perfectly content.

Cade rubbed behind her ears and the purring settled into a deep rumble. "I had an old and grumpy cat just like Mogs before I got the kitten."

Quinn was afraid to ask. "What happened to it?"

"He died of old age. The cat was the same age as me. He was in my last foster home. They didn't want him, so I took Tigs with me when I left. I missed having a cat so I got another tabby kitten."

"Charlie."

"Yeah." Cade sounded heartbroken.

If Cade had been his boy, Quinn would have wrapped himself around him, to comfort him. But he wasn't, and there was a line Quinn couldn't cross.

Cade

Cade needed to be held so much it hurt. It was one of the things he really missed about Eric, at least the way he'd been in the beginning. There had come a point when Cade had begun to dread his embrace because of what followed. He pushed those memories from his mind. Maybe when he returned from London, he could get a new cat.

"Cade."

He looked up, not realizing for a moment Quinn was so close. "Yes?"

Had Quinn understood how much he needed a hug?

"We need to work out a plan for the next two weeks."

Disappointment slammed into Cade like a freight train, and he lashed out. "My management company has the details. I haven't got time to waste on trivialities with the muscle." He took pleasure in seeing Quinn's expression darken. "I've got work to do."

"You cleared your schedule for today."

"Yeah, well, now it's uncleared."

He stalked out of the kitchen and headed toward the studio. He hoped, he prayed Quinn would call him back, discipline him for being a grade A brat, but nothing happened. A tear ran down his cheek and he dashed it away angrily. He wasn't going to give Quinn the satisfaction of seeing him cry. He was the client. He was an adult. He was a boy without a Daddy. He didn't need a goddamn cat.

* * *

Cade stood in the middle of the studio, not really sure what to do. He was prepared for the event next week. The band was getting together because they loved playing, and any excuse was better than not being loud and noisy.

But he was on his own, and the idea of playing the songs for the gig didn't really appeal to him. Cade picked up his acoustic guitar and sat down on a stool. He picked out a chord. He hated when he was like this, his mind jumping all over the place, anger coursing through his veins. He used to be like this as a kid, acting out. It wouldn't be long before he'd find himself moving to a new home because they couldn't handle him, as he wasn't a 'good' kid. More tears threatened to spill but he forced them back. That part of his life was over. He'd moved on and this was his home. He didn't have to be good for anyone. Certainly not for muscle he barely knew.

He picked out the chords to a song he'd written when he was fourteen and lost in his own head, scared of knowing he was gay and anyone finding out. He snorted. Being gay was the least of his worries, although he didn't know that then.

Cade closed his eyes and started to play, muscle memory taking over as he played a tune he hadn't thought of in years, fumbling a little at the words, but the notes etched in his mind forever. He came to the end too soon, flattening his palm against the strings.

"That was beautiful."

Struggling to come back to the real world, he opened his eyes at Quinn's praise. "It was crap." He was always brutally honest about his music and art.

Quinn stood in the doorway of the studio. Cade hadn't heard him come in: he'd been so lost in his music. Even in his fugue state he still couldn't miss how gorgeous Quinn was, tall and broad-shouldered, lean waist and long legs. When he'd turned up in leather at CDR, Cade could have come on the spot.

"No," Quinn contradicted, "it was heartfelt. I'll leave you to your practice. I just wanted to check you were okay."

Cade wanted to snarl, to tell him to fuck off, just to see what reaction he'd get. But instead he managed a short "Thanks."

Quinn nodded and vanished, closing the door with a quiet snap, leaving Cade staring, wondering what just happened there.

"Keep it together, Connolly," he muttered.

He stayed in the studio until his fingertips were bleeding, and his stomach growled at him loud enough that he remembered he hadn't eaten that day. It didn't matter. That was what takeout was for.

The aroma that greeted him as he walked toward the kitchen made his belly almost cramp, it smelled so good.

Quinn looked up from stirring a large pan of red sauce as he walked in. "Good. I was about to fetch you."

"You cook?" Cade bent down to scratch Mogs who'd appeared with a chirrup. She stalked away and curled up in a small nest of blankets, clearly satisfied with the attention she'd received.

"I like cooking," Quinn said. "I don't get much opportunity being on the road. I always cook at home. I was making pasta for myself tonight, so I brought it with me."

"I'm a vegetarian."

"I know. I checked the file. I am too."

Cade stared at him. "You?"

Quinn chuckled. "You expected me to eat steak and all the fixin's?"

"Well, yeah."

"I make a mean baked potato," Quinn assured him. "Now wash your hands and sit down."

Wash his hands? Was he five?

"Yes, Mom," he said snidely.

Then he caught the fire in Quinn's eyes and swallowed. Oh shit, he'd woken the Daddy, and Daddy was not pleased.

"Wash your hands or you don't get dinner," Quinn said.

Cade raised an eyebrow. "You know this is my house, right? I can call for takeout."

"Last chance, Cade."

Quinn turned back to stir the sauce. He didn't even wait to see if Cade obeyed. That was more mortifying than if he'd stood there, watching what Cade would do. He expected Cade to obey him.

Cade chewed on his bottom lip. Dammit. He went to the sink and did as he was told. Not because he wanted to obey Quinn, but he was so hungry.

"Good boy," Quinn praised as Cade dried his hands.

"Not your boy," Cade said automatically, but inwardly he glowed under the praise.

Quinn ignored that. "Sit down. I'm going to deliver the team's dinners and I'll be back."

"You cooked for the security team?"

"Of course. It's a long day for them."

He said it so matter of factly, Cade just blinked. Quinn was not like any bodyguard he'd ever had before. All the bodyguards he met lived on takeout. Quinn was a Daddy, which made the nurturing aspect understandable but even so, he'd never met a bodyguard who cooked.

Quinn picked up four covered plates and flatware and left the kitchen. Cade sat there, stomach rumbling from the delicious aroma. He was tempted to serve himself, but he didn't want to imagine the consequences if he did.

He heard voices, then the sound of the door shutting again. Quinn returned and went to wash his hands.

"I'm really hungry," Cade said plaintively.

"Me too," Quinn confessed, then he frowned. "Have you eaten today?"

"No. I was too anxious this morning, and we blew through lunch."

Quinn dished up a large plate of pasta and put it in front of Cade. "That won't happen again. You'll be eating three meals a day."

"I don't eat breakfast," Cade mumbled around a mouthful of pasta. "Christ, this is good."

Quinn's glower deepened. "You'll eat breakfast while you're in my charge."

"I really don't want food when I get up."

"How long are you going to be in the studio tomorrow?" Quinn demanded.

Cade shrugged. "Eight, ten hours."

"You'll eat before you go in, and I'll provide lunch for you and the band."

"It's really not—"

The growl told Cade to shut the hell up. He focused on his pasta. It was really very good.

Chapter Four

Quinn

Quinn watched in approval as Cade shoveled down a second helping of pasta smothered in Quinn's grandpa's secret sauce. The boy was too skinny and now that he'd found out Cade forgot to eat, Quinn understood why.

"More?" he asked, as Cade sat back in his seat and rubbed his belly.

"I couldn't eat another mouthful," Cade confessed. "That sauce was amazing. Where did you buy it?"

"I made it. My grandpa's recipe."

"Wow, I can't remember the last time I had a home-cooked meal." Cade furrowed his brow as if he was trying to pin it down.

"Strada didn't cook for you?"

"Eric didn't cook. We ate out or got takeout. I didn't mind. I was busy all the time." Cade obviously didn't realize how wistful he sounded or the longing glances he shot at the remaining pasta.

Quinn had to hold back his growl. Cooking was one of the things he loved doing for his boys, even those who were just passing through. He'd always fed and nurtured them. Just exactly what had Strada brought to their relationship except his fists and cock?

"I'll make meals to put in your freezer. You'll have home-cooked food when you come back from London."

"You don't have to."

"I want to," Quinn insisted. "If we had time, I'd teach you to cook."

Cade shook his head. "I'm hopeless at cooking. Eric tried to make me cook until he realized it was hopeless and quit spanking my ass."

The growl came then. Quinn couldn't hold it back.

"Quinn?" Cade asked uncertainly.

"Teaching my boys to cook is one of my greatest pleasures. I don't spank them for bad meals. That's my failure for not showing you properly. When we cook together, you'll be rewarded for getting it right."

It was only Cade's comically wide eyes that made him realize he'd gone from 'my boys' to 'you', and suggested he would be around to teach Cade. He huffed and ended with a lame, "My boys like cooking."

The silence stretched out between them until Cade spoke. "I'd like that."

Like what? Being taught how to cook? Or being Quinn's boy?

"Cade—"

Cade got to his feet. "I need to sleep."

He went to leave the kitchen, but fortunately Quinn's brain caught up with what was happening.

"Take your plate to the dishwasher."

Cade turned at the order. "What?"

"You need to take your plate to the dishwasher."

"But—"

"Plate. Dishwasher. Now," Quinn said flatly.

Cade looked astonished. "This is my house."

"I'm not your servant."

"I'm your client."

"I cooked for you, and I expect you to help me clear up."

Quinn waited to see what Cade would do. Was he going to obey, or would he balk? Judging by the look on Cade's face, it could go either way. Cade scowled at him, his fists clenching, then he picked up his bowl, and stomped over to the dishwasher to put it in. Quinn winced at the force he used, hoping the bowl didn't shatter. Cade stomped out of the kitchen, and Quinn let him go, although it went against every instinct in him.

He looked at the way the bowl was jammed in the dishwasher. It was obvious Cade had never loaded it before. Had Strada done that or did he have a maid? Quinn made a note on his phone to ask Dominic about it, if Cade was still throwing a tantrum tomorrow. Then he finished loading the dishwasher and set it going, placed the leftover food in a storage container to go in the fridge when it was cool enough, and made himself a coffee. If Cade wanted one, he'd have to come back into the kitchen.

He needed to call his friend in San Francisco, but it wasn't a conversation he wanted Cade to overhear. He'd wait until Cade was settled in the studio before he called Leo.

First, he needed to find his errant client. From the noise, he was sure Cade had gone up the stairs, but he would check once he'd made sure all the windows and doors were locked. He also checked in with Tormac, who ran the evening team, and whistled to Mogs who opened one eye, got up lazily and stretched one leg at a time. Then he scooped her under his arm, flicked off the lights, and headed upstairs. He saw a light under Cade's door plus he heard noise that sounded like a movie from the gunfire and explosions.

Quinn did the same check on the second floor to make sure all the windows were locked. Then he knocked on Cade's door. There was a sudden silence as the movie was muted, but nothing else happened. He contemplated knocking again when the door opened.

"Hey." Cade was dressed in plaid pajama pants and a tight white T-shirt.

Quinn nearly swallowed his tongue. The T-shirt exposed the ink and showed off the tight compact muscles that had been hidden before. The urge to throw Cade on the bed, strip off his clothes, and follow those muscles with his tongue was one he was going to have to keep in check.

"Just making sure you're okay," he said.

Cade avoided his eyes. "I'm fine."

Quinn waited, but Cade didn't say anything else. "I need to check your windows, then I'll leave you alone."

Cade stepped back. "Be my guest."

On impulse, Quinn handed him Mogs who chirruped happily at being in Cade's arms, then he checked the windows and the balcony doors. Satisfied, he turned back to find Cade on the bed, Mogs nestled in the crook of his crossed legs.

He sighed. "Have I lost my cat?"

Cade gave him an oddly sweet but also mischievous grin. "Maybe."

"I'm going to bed. If she becomes a pain dump her in with me."

"She'll be fine," Cade said, scratching behind her ears.

Maybe he was a little piqued that Mogs obviously preferred Cade to the man who had fed her for the past fourteen years, but he'd get over it...in time. Whatever kept his client calm worked for him. He said goodnight and shut the door behind him.

In his own room he checked in with the team once more.

"It's fine. Same as it was five minutes ago," Tormac snarked.

"Call me—"

"Yeah, yeah." Tormac disconnected the call.

"Fuck you too," Quinn said easily and put his phone on the nightstand. He knew he drove the security team nuts with his obsession for detail.

He stripped down to his briefs, grabbed his phone, and headed into the bathroom for a shower. It had been a long day and he needed a few minutes to unwind. The shower was fierce against the tight muscles of his shoulders, and he spent longer in there than he'd intended, groaning in pleasure at the feel of the hot water pounding on his back. When he was in danger of leaning against the tiles and falling asleep, he investigated the bottles lined up on the small shelf since he'd left his toiletries in the bedroom. He grabbed a shampoo he vaguely recognized and squeezed a dollop into his palm, inhaling the citrusy aroma. It was a pleasure to massage it into his scalp. It would have been better to have someone else do it. Quinn pushed away the thought of his cheek pressed into Cade's belly as Cade massaged his hair and he sucked on Cade's cock.

Not. Going. There.

But the image in his head was breathtaking, and his body reacted accordingly. Quinn soaped himself down and finished his shower before his cock begged for a happy ending. He grabbed a towel and roughly dried himself off before wrapping it around his waist and walking into the bedroom.

To find Cade sitting on the bed, Mogs in the well of his crossed legs again.

He thanked God he'd wrapped the towel around his waist rather than going naked as he usually did.

"Cade."

"Shame." The boy looked far too pleased with himself. Had he hoped to catch Quinn like this?

Quinn folded his arms across his chest. "You want something?"

There was a long pause. Too long.

Cade's lips twitched.

Oh, you are begging for a spanking, my boy.

Quinn raised an eyebrow. Cade huffed. "Mogs wanted to sleep with you. Your door was shut."

"So you thought you'd wait with her?"

"I didn't want her to get lonely."

Quinn gave a derisive grunt.

Cade sighed. "Okay, I... just needed to reassure myself you were here. I don't sleep well at the moment."

Quinn's annoyance faded away. "Have you been on your own since you threw him out?"

Cade focused his attention on Mogs. "Yeah. I spend most nights in the studio working on new songs. I worry... if I relax... I might wake up and find Eric staring at me. He used to do that."

He didn't say what happened then, but his tone was grim enough that Quinn could guess.

Christ, how many times had that happened when they were together? No wonder the boy was exhausted. Quinn was going to change that. Cade needed sleep.

"Come on, let's get you to bed," he said. "I'll stay with you until you fall asleep."

"You don't—"

"I do," Quinn insisted. "It's my job to take care of you and that's what I'm going to do. Wait a minute while I change into pajamas."

He rummaged in his pack for a T-shirt and pajama bottoms, ignoring the whispered, "Too bad," behind him as he went into the bathroom. He used the towel to get rid of the last remaining drops and dressed, roughly drying his hair before he left the bathroom.

Cade lifted Mogs, crooning at her to soothe her grumbles. She swiftly settled when he kept her in his arms. Quinn knew Mogs had probably been fine with Cade, but he wasn't going to call the boy out on it.

The last one to leave the bedroom, Quinn took a pillow from the bed and flicked the switch, plunging the room into darkness. He wasn't coming back here tonight.

Cade

Going to Quinn's room had been on a whim, Cade's inner brat coming out to play. When he'd found Quinn was in the bathroom he'd been torn, unsure whether to leave Mogs or stay. Some impulse made him stay. When Quinn had come out of the bathroom wearing only a towel and with droplets peppered across tanned shoulders, Cade had to fight the overwhelming urge to beg Quinn to allow him to lick off each drop, followed by him falling to his knees to lick the line of Quinn's abs.

He'd only intended to wind up Quinn, dial up the brattiness. He'd never intended to actually spill his guts about his inner fears. What was it about Quinn that made him cough up his innermost thoughts?

Now he headed back to his bedroom, Mogs in his arms, and Quinn close behind. What the hell was Quinn going to do? Sit there and stare at him until he fell asleep? He turned in the bedroom, uncertain of what Quinn expected.

Quinn tossed the pillow on the floor, took Mogs out of his arms and nodded at the bed. "Climb in and I'll give you Mogs when you're settled."

"What are you going to do?" Cade asked.

"Stay with you until you fall asleep."

"Then what?"

"I'm going to sleep down here." Quinn pointed at the pillow next to the bed.

"You can't do that," Cade protested.

"Are you questioning my decisions?" Quinn glowered at him.

"I'll be all right."

Cade had planned to sneak down to the studio as soon as Quinn was asleep. If he hadn't gone to Quinn's bedroom, he could have done that. Now how was he going to get past him? Maybe when he was asleep...

"I'm a very light sleeper," Quinn assured him. "Any movement will disturb me."

Cade held back a groan. Now he was going to spend the night staring at the ceiling, trapped in his bedroom by the muscleman. Even if it was his own fault. He slid into bed, feeling resentful and touched at the same time. He'd never met a bodyguard who insisted on taking care of him... like a Daddy. Quinn was a Daddy. Still, Daddies could be a pain in the butt, particularly when boys couldn't sleep.

Mogs settled with a purr as Quinn placed her on the bed and Cade snuggled around her. He looked up to see

Quinn smiling at them. It was a tender expression for such a hard man, and it warmed Cade.

Quinn switched off the main light. "Close your eyes and see if you can sleep."

Cade licked his lips. "I don't like the dark."

Immediately the lamp on the nightstand cast a warm glow over the room.

"Thank you," he said, as Quinn resumed his seat.

"You're welcome," Quinn rumbled.

Cade felt he should explain but looking at Quinn's gentle expression he knew he didn't need to. Quinn understood.

He rolled over and cuddled around Mogs. There was no way he could sleep like this, with Quinn in the room. He was acutely aware of the huge man on the floor next to him, the soft sounds of his breathing as he tried to make himself comfortable.

He rolled over to look at Quinn who had his eyes closed. "Quinn."

Quinn opened his eyes, and blinked, long lashes Cade hadn't noticed sweeping his cheeks. "Yes?"

"I can't sleep."

"It's been five minutes," Quinn pointed out.

"Maybe I'll go down to the studio," Cade suggested.

Quinn sighed and sat up. "You need to sleep."

"I never sleep."

"How about you scoot over to the other side of the bed, and I'll sleep where you are. Then you'll know I'm here, and you can relax."

Cade stared at him. Did Quinn really think his presence would erase weeks of insomnia? Ego much.

"Would that scare you?" Quinn asked.

"No," Cade muttered and moved over.

Quinn sat on the bed. "Are you sure, Cade? I don't want to frighten you."

"It won't scare me," Cade lied, even though he was suddenly terrified at the thought of having another man in bed with him.

There was one advantage though. Quinn wasn't between him and the door. When Quinn was asleep he could slip out of bed and tip-toe out of the bedroom.

Quinn got on the bed and lay down but didn't make a move to get under the covers.

"Get under the comforter or you'll get cold," Cade said.

"Okay."

Quinn slid gently under the cover. Mogs chirruped a couple of times and took time to settle. Her presence was comforting. Like a cat could protect him if Quinn decided to attack him.

"Cade, it's okay. I'm not going to hurt you."

Cade blinked. "What?"

"You're shaking," Quinn said.

"I am?" He hadn't realized.

"Do you want me to get out of bed?"

Yes. No. Yes

Cade had no idea what he wanted.

"No."

"Okay, then. Good night." Quinn sighed and settled again.

Silence again. Cade stared at the balcony door. Was it locked? Could Eric climb up to the first floor?

"Cade," Quinn said.

"Yes?"

"You're safe with me. I won't hurt you."

"That's what he said to me. Right before he...he..." Cade's voice cracked, and he blinked away unshed tears.

"I'm here to protect you from Strada."

Cade let out a sigh that felt as if it was drawn from his toes. "I know."

"But you're still scared."

"I'm scared all the time," Cade confessed. "I expect him to leap out from behind every corner."

"I understand."

"You do?" Cade asked doubtfully.

"Cade, you've been violated by a man who should have protected you from the world."

"I thought for the first time I had someone...family. But he hurt me. Daddy hurt me."

And then he was howling, unable to hold back the tears. He expected Quinn to grab him, try to hug him, and was ready to put up a fight. But nothing happened. Quinn stayed where he was. Cade howled and cried until he had nothing left inside him, until the crying went to sobbing and finally to shuddering breaths.

"Do you need water?" Quinn said when Cade was quiet.

"Please." Cade felt empty, his eyes stung and his throat was raw. "There's a fridge in the corner by the window."

He felt the bed dip and Quinn went over to the fridge and pulled out a bottle of water. Cade sat up and took the uncapped bottle from him. He drank, needing the cool water to slip down his throat, to soothe the pain he'd been bottling up inside.

Quinn sat back on the bed, his silent warrior, ready to take care of him.

Cade looked at him. "I'm sorry."

"Have you seen a therapist?"

"What?" That was the last question Cade expected.

"Since you split up. Have you seen a therapist?"

Cade shook his head. "I've been preparing for this event. I haven't had time."

"This is only a suggestion. I can't make you go. But I think you should talk with a therapist."

"And tell them what? My Daddy liked beating me up? Yeah, I can just see how that will go down. It'll be all over social media before I leave the building."

"There is such a thing as patient confidentiality," Quinn said mildly.

Cade snorted.

"I know a couple of therapists from our world. I'll give you their numbers."

"They understand about Daddies and boys?" Cade asked doubtfully.

Quinn's lips twitched. "One's a Daddy and the other one is a little."

Cade's mouth dropped open. "Really?"

"Really. They're both good. I've recommended them before."

"I'll think about it."

He was making no promises, especially not when he was exhausted to the bone. He yawned and lay down. Mogs mewed in his ear.

Quinn chuckled. "She just wants to check you're okay."

Cade rolled over to face her and scratched under her chin. He was acutely aware of Quinn watching him but he focused his attention on the cat.

"Thank you," he said after a few minutes.

"For what?"

"Not trying to hold me."

"You're not ready for that," Quinn said.

"I don't think I'll ever be ready." Tears prickled at the back of his eyes and he blinked rapidly, determined not to break down again. Then he yawned. "God, I'm so fucking tired."

"Go to sleep," Quinn suggested. Or was it an order?

Cade thought he'd close his eyes for a moment. They were so sore. He could go down to the studio in five or ten minutes.

Chapter Five

Quinn

He watched Cade sleep for at least thirty minutes. The boy had fallen into a deep sleep almost as soon as he closed his eyes. Quinn wasn't stupid. Cade was hopeless at hiding his emotions. He knew Cade had planned to sneak out of the bedroom as soon as Quinn was asleep. Where would he go? Probably the studio. Quinn had warned him, but he didn't think Cade had taken it on board. If Cade put one foot on the ground, he would know. If he didn't wake up, his furry alarm clock would make a noise. Unlike the night before, Quinn was clear-headed. It was a relief not to flop into bed fueled with whiskey. He never drank while on the job or dealing with a boy in distress.

Cade didn't move the whole time Quinn watched him. He was dead to the world. How long had he gone without sleep? Who the hell was taking care of him? Where was the community? The Daddy community was very small. Someone should have been here all the time to pick up the pieces when Cade fell apart. He was going to chew the asses of some of his friends tomorrow.

Quinn needed sleep himself. Cade might only sleep for an hour or two, or he might sleep for the night. Whatever, tomorrow was going to be another long day. Quinn stroked Mogs who stretched lazily and grabbed his hand with her front paws when he tried to move away. He smiled and left his hand where it was.

* * *

Quinn woke once in the night, mentally putting the pieces together. He was in Cade Connolly's bedroom, in his bed. What had woken him up? Was Cade trying to sneak away? He opened his eyes to find Mogs still between them and Cade on his back, arms and legs spread out almost like a starfish. Quinn smiled, the smile fading when he heard Cade make a distressed sound. Cade frowned, his mouth twisting and his arms lifting in front of him.

"No, Eric, don't! I didn't smile at him. Please...don't hurt me!"

Quinn sucked in a breath. Cade was having a nightmare, and Quinn didn't need to be drawn a diagram about the content.

He leaned closer but he didn't touch the boy. "Cade. Cade. It's okay. You're safe. Go back to sleep."

Cade's face screwed up as if he were confused. "Safe? You promise?"

Quinn growled under his breath. All his boys were safe in his care. "You're safe, Cade. Go back to sleep. Eric can't hurt you again."

A single tear ran from the corner of Cade's eye, down

his temple, to soak into the pillow. "He promised not to hurt me, but he did. Over and over. He hurt me."

"I know," Quinn said. "But I won't hurt you. I promise you're safe with me."

Cade let out a long sigh, rolled over toward him, put his hands under his cheek like a child, and fell asleep again.

Quinn rolled onto his back and stared up at the ceiling, contemplating all the ways he could hurt Eric Strada.

Cade

Cade groaned as he opened his eyes. He was shocked to find sunlight playing through a gap in the drapes across the comforter. He'd spent all night in his bed. So much for sneaking out. Yet, he felt exhausted from bones to balls. Worse than he had after nights of no sleep. Then he remembered his breakdown the previous night.

Oh God.

He'd lost it completely in front of Quinn.

Cade turned his head to find Mogs staring at him but no sign of Quinn. She'd curled up on Quinn's pillow as if she was guarding Cade. "What did I do, Mogs? I made a complete idiot of myself."

She chirruped at him as if in agreement.

He pulled a face. "You're not supposed to agree, old girl."

Another chirrup and a sniff.

Cade put his arm across his eyes, blocking out her judgmental expression. Trust Quinn to have a cat more judgmental than he was. "You're right. I needed it."

He'd suppressed the need to cry for so long. It wasn't that he believed the 'men don't cry' bullcrap. It was more complicated than that. Cade preferred emotional outbursts within the confines of his relationship with his Daddy. He knew his Daddy could handle it, handle him. Without a Daddy, he was adrift.

"I can handle it myself."

"You can," Quinn agreed, making Cade jump, "but you don't have to be alone. I'm here. That's my job."

Cade felt his cheeks burn. Was he forever destined to make a complete idiot of himself in front of Quinn?

"Breakfast is ready," Quinn said.

Cade sat bolt upright, panic flooding through him. "What's the time?"

"Six. You've got time for a shower and breakfast before your band arrives."

Cade stared at him. "You made me breakfast?"

Quinn leaned against the door frame. He wore a well-worn pale gray Henley, and jeans which should have been illegal from the way they hugged his ass and package.

Cade dragged his gaze back to Quinn's face. "I don't eat breakfast."

"You do today." There it was again. That calm belief that Cade would do whatever he told him to.

Cade shook his head. Quinn was not going to win every battle. "I don't eat breakfast."

"Then you don't go into the studio."

Cade's jaw dropped. "Who the hell do you think you are? You don't get to make that decision."

"I'm the bodyguard who's going to get you through the next two weeks."

"You protect my ass. Not force-feed me."

Quinn didn't move a muscle. "Get your ass downstairs, and you're gonna eat. You don't get to choose."

"You're fired."

"Whatever. After breakfast."

Cade clambered to his knees, for once not paying any attention to Mogs's disgruntled huff as he disturbed her. "Are you listening to me?"

Quinn drove him nuts. He just stood there like Cade was a small, annoying kid.

Because you're behaving like one.

Cade growled at himself. "What's for breakfast?"

"Fruit, oatmeal, yogurt, nuts," Quinn said.

That didn't sound too bad. "Coffee?"

"Of course. And juice."

He sighed. "Okay."

Cade took satisfaction in seeing Quinn's look of surprise. Okay, so another time he might have made more of a tantrum, but today he was too tired to care.

"Have I got time to shower first?"

Quinn shook his head. "Eat first."

Damn, he wasn't going to get out of it.

Cade slung his robe around his shoulders and stalked out of the bedroom, Mogs hard on his heels. Quinn followed him at a slower pace.

He rocked back on his heels when he walked into the kitchen. The counter was laden with food. He turned to stare at Quinn. "How many are you cooking for?"

"I've got breakfast for us, the two teams, and your band. Don't worry, I'll replace the food."

Cade waved his hand absently. "It's okay. I'm just not used to seeing so much food in my kitchen."

"I'll clear it away at the end. Which reminds me, when is your housekeeper due in?"

"What housekeeper?"

Quinn furrowed his brow. "You don't have a housekeeper?"

Cade licked his lips. "I never wanted anyone to find out about me."

"Who cleans the house?"

"I do. Eric made me clean it every week. He said it would keep me grounded. I've let it go since he left."

He'd loved and hated cleaning house. Eric seemed to know what chores to give to focus him. At the same time, he wanted to paint or play music.

"You need to focus on the event, not cleaning. I'll take that over," Quinn said. "If you feel scattered or unfocused, and I don't notice, talk to me. We can find you something to do."

"I like drawing," Cade confessed.

"Does it help you to focus?" At Cade's nod, Quinn said, "I'll make sure you have time to draw every day."

Cade gave him a wry smile. "It's going to be manic for the next two weeks. I won't have time to breathe, let alone draw."

"You leave it with me. Sit." Quinn pointed to a chair then ladled something into a dish.

Cade sat with a huff. Quinn put a small bowl of oatmeal in front of him.

"I don't like—"

"Eat. Put fruit and whatever you like in it, but you're going to eat the oatmeal."

Cade scowled down at the bowl. It wasn't that he didn't like oatmeal. It was that he didn't like being made to eat it. It reminded him of the food in foster care. He doctored the oatmeal with strawberries, whipped cream, and sugar. He waited for Quinn to say something, but Quinn was busy piling food onto a tray.

"I'm surprised you're not cooking pancakes and bacon," Cade said before he took his first mouthful of oatmeal.

"They'll eat whatever I give them," Quinn said. Then he grinned. "They'd prefer the pancakes, but I told them to quit complaining."

Cade laughed. Then choked as a piece of strawberry went down the wrong way. By the time he'd finished coughing, blown his nose, and wiped his eyes, Quinn had delivered breakfast to the security teams.

He scowled as Quinn came back into the kitchen. "You're supposed to be taking care of me."

"You're still breathing, aren't you?" Quinn said indifferently. He sat next to Cade with a larger bowl of oatmeal which he ate plain.

"That's not the point," Cade protested.

"I knew you were fine. I gave you tissue to blow your nose. I know how to give the Heimlich maneuver if necessary."

"I hate you," Cade muttered. And drank his coffee, hating Quinn and the world. Even Mogs had been more interested in her breakfast than making sure he was all right.

But he calmed bit by bit, and nibbled on more fruit, although he ignored the yogurt.

"Where did you get the food from?" he asked.

"I asked the day team to bring it, with the promise of breakfast. As we're going to be based here while you rehearse, we needed to stock up."

"I have someone who delivers usually."

Quinn shook his head. His chin caught on the spoon and a little oatmeal lodged in his stubble. Cade didn't tell him. "I don't want outsiders coming here."

"I know them," Cade pointed out.

"I know you do, but I'm betting Strada does too."

"You think he's going to poison the delivery?"

Quinn smiled. "No, but he could try to deliver a note to

you."

Cade stared down at his empty bowl. "He tried that in the beginning. Before things got nasty."

"Okay, so no delivery drivers. And that includes Toxic Tessie's flowers."

"Who?" Cade felt like he'd missed part of the conversation.

"Your superfan. She can save her money or buy someone else carnations."

"She'll be devastated," Cade said.

"She is receiving a visit today from Dominic who is going to explain that now is not a good time to contact you."

"Are you sure that's wise?" Cade was only partly joking. He'd seen what happened when stars rejected their super-fans. He never wanted to be on the receiving end of Batty Brenda's wrath.

"It's wise," Quinn said grimly.

Cade grinned as the doorbell echoed throughout the house and Quinn nearly shed his skin again.

"Jesus," Quinn muttered.

Cade snickered as Quinn stalked to the door. He heard the familiar bellows of Keith, his drummer, as he barged in, and the quieter tones of his bass guitarist, Dave. The two of them were like apples and oranges.

Keith's eyes lit up as he saw the breakfast spread over the counter. "Tell me some of that is for us." He filled a bowl with oatmeal.

"He's not a pig, unlike you," Dave said, shoving Keith aside so he could hug Cade.

Cade was fully aware of Quinn watching them from the doorway. He returned Dave's hug, but he knew Quinn relaxed a fraction when Dave stepped back and headed over to inspect what was left of the breakfast. *Interesting.*

"Where's Ian?" he asked.

"The fucker overslept," Keith said around a mouthful of oatmeal, spraying it all over Dave who leapt back, cursing at him.

Cade sighed. "Sorry, Quinn. I forgot to tell you these guys are pigs."

Keith grinned and it was really a disgusting sight, oatmeal mashed into his teeth. "Ya got me, baby."

Cade shook his head and grinned at Quinn. "I need to get ready."

He got up, went to walk away, caught Quinn's scowl, and picked up his plate to take over to the dishwasher. When he turned, he caught Quinn's approving nod and Dave's speculative glance. Dammit, he knew Dave was going to be asking questions.

Quinn followed him up the stairs, and Cade swore he was so close he could feel Quinn's breath on the back of his neck.

At the bedroom door, Cade turned to Quinn. "You don't need to come with me. I can dress myself. I'm a big boy now."

It was meant to be a light-hearted quip, but his voice went a little breathy on the 'boy', and Quinn's eyes darkened. Their gazes locked and Cade knew what Quinn was thinking about, because he was thinking exactly the same thing.

Cade made a noise in the back of his throat. Quinn reached out and stroked one finger from his jaw and down his neck.

"I...you..." Cade started.

The crash of something from downstairs made them both jump.

Quinn shook his head as if he were waking up. "Get

showered and be back downstairs in ten minutes."

"I take longer than that," Cade scoffed.

"Ten minutes," Quinn insisted.

"Or?"

He knew poking a sleeping tiger was never good, but he wanted to see what Quinn would do.

"Boys who disobey me always get disciplined."

Cade bit his lip. "I'm not your boy."

"As far as your friends are concerned, you are."

"They don't know about the Daddy/boy relationship. They think you're my fussy, over-protective boyfriend."

"Then they won't be surprised when I drag you out of the shower. Nine minutes."

"I don't have to obey you."

"Quit pushing me and get showered."

Cade stared into eyes the color of melted chocolate. The desire to push and push until Quinn snapped was overwhelming. If the guys hadn't been in the kitchen he would have. They both knew it.

Quinn bent down until his lips almost brushed Cade's. "You don't have to act out to get what you want."

"What do I have to do?"

"Just. Ask."

Cade sucked in a breath. He took a step back and would have fallen onto the stairs, but Quinn grabbed and steadied him. Even now he didn't try to hug or cuddle him.

"Go on," Quinn said. "Eight minutes."

Cade growled and headed for the bathroom. He was halfway there when he suddenly realized Quinn had smacked his ass. Barely more than a pat and not enough to sting, but nevertheless. He turned but Quinn was gone. He was going to have words with his muscle—in seven minutes time.

Chapter Six

Quinn

It had been so hard to let Cade go shower by himself. Quinn hovered at the bottom of the stairs, between Cade and the rest of the world. Cade reappeared seven and a half minutes later still toweling his hair and wearing his T-shirt inside out.

"Good boy," Quinn praised him. "Although you might want to turn your T-shirt around the other way."

"Not your boy," Cade said automatically, but Quinn saw the flash of pleasure in his eyes before he stripped off his shirt. Quinn couldn't tear his gaze away from the nipple rings, the ink across one shoulder, stretching down his back and curling around his side. Between the ink and the treasure trail down his slender belly, Quinn wanted to pick Cade up in his arms and take him to bed.

"You like dragons," he said.

"Yeah." Cade's voice was muffled as he slid the cotton over his head. He ran his hands through his hair and looked up at Quinn. "Better?"

Quinn liked the fact Cade sought his approval, even though he didn't have to. "Better."

They walked back into the kitchen to find Dave picking at the last of the fresh berries, and Keith on the phone, his face set in a scowl.

"Where's Ian?" Cade asked.

"Keith's talking to him now," Dave said.

Keith held the phone away from his ear. "Some fucker's slashed his tires."

Quinn frowned. "His car?"

"His bike. He's gonna get a car here."

"Give me the phone," Quinn ordered. Keith handed it over without a word. "Ian, this is Quinn. Give me your address, and I'll send someone to get you."

He put the address in a text message to Doug and sent it to him with a request he investigate the slashed tires. He wouldn't put it past Strada to target the band just to inconvenience Cade. Doug returned the message with a thumbs up.

Quinn handed the phone back to Keith and looked at the band. "He'll be here soon."

Cade smiled but the smile didn't reach his eyes. "Guys, go in the studio. I'll be there in five."

Dave studied Cade for a moment, then he steered Keith away from the remains of the breakfast, despite his loud protests, and out of the kitchen.

Cade turned to Quinn. "Do you think the slashed tires had something to do with Eric?"

"I don't know," Quinn admitted, "but I'm not taking any chances."

"Thanks for taking care of my friends too."

Quinn nodded. It was part of his job, but the praise felt good. He was used to being in the background and ignored, except when they needed his help. He liked the control he had this time. Cade hesitated, then he vanished after Dave and Keith.

Their voices faded as the studio door closed behind them. Quinn took a deep breath, knowing Cade was safely installed in the studio for the rest of the day. His phone buzzed and he checked the screen. Ian was fifteen minutes out. Quinn took his time clearing up the kitchen. He needed to make a phone call, but he didn't want to risk Cade overhearing. The dishwasher was loaded and the counters clear when he heard Doug's voice.

"Quinn?"

Quinn walked out to the entry, hand on his holster, but relaxed when he saw the man standing next to Doug.

"Ian. Good to see you."

The young guy was the antithesis of Cade. He looked as if he'd stepped off a Californian beach with his surfboard rather than a member of a pop band. His long, streaked by the sun, blond hair flowed around his shoulders and his skin was a sun-kissed tan all year around. From Quinn's memory, he was that color all over. He wore baggy shorts and a large shirt. Quinn hadn't put two and two together when he saw his name.

Ian turned with a huge smile. "Hey, sir. Great to see you. I thought that was you on the phone, but you disconnected before I could ask."

Doug's eyebrows raised at the 'sir'. Quinn ignored him. He reached out a hand to shake Ian's but found himself with an armful of Ian and a mouthful of blond hair.

"Why are you mauling my boyfriend?"

Quinn turned, still holding onto Ian and looked into Cade's icy-cold gaze.

Still clutching Quinn, Ian beamed at Cade. "I didn't

realize you got yourself a new Daddy. You lucky boy. Daddy Quinn's one of the best."

If anything, Cade's scowl deepened. "You know each other?"

Ian didn't seem to notice the drop in temperature. "A long time ago." He tilted his head to look up at Quinn. "I haven't seen you for, what? Four years?"

Quinn extricated himself from Ian's grasp. "Something like that. I didn't realize Ian was your guitarist."

Ian pouted at being let go, but Quinn fixed him with a stern look, and he subsided.

Cade grunted and turned on his heel to stalk back to the studio. Ian finally realized he'd put both feet in it and grimaced at Quinn, mouthing "Sorry," before he hurried after Cade.

"Oh brother, are you in trouble," Doug snickered.

Quinn sighed. "You have no idea. Ian's a lovely guy, but he's got no filters. I'll be lucky if Cade's even talking to me by the end of the day."

"Were you and he...?"

"Together?" Quinn shook his head. "We played together a few times, but he wanted something different from me. He wanted a 24/7 Daddy/boy relationship, and I could never be that for him. Work took me away too much. He's fun though, and has the biggest heart I've ever met."

"Really."

Unseen by Cade, Quinn closed his eyes in a wince. Did Cade have to come back at that moment?

"I'm out of here," Doug muttered and vanished out of the front door.

Coward!

Quinn turned to face Cade, who glared at him furiously. "Okay, what are you most angry about? The fact he hugged me or that we've played together in the past?"

Cade chewed on his bottom lip. "You're supposed to be my fake boyfriend and I find you hugging him."

"He hugged me," Quinn said, "but it was only to say hello. I haven't seen him for over four years."

"You like them young?" Cade snapped.

Quinn stiffened. "I only play with men over twenty-one. Check with Ian if you don't believe me."

Cade curled his lip, but he didn't respond. Quinn felt rage flood through him, and he fought to control it. His reputation in the Daddy community was one of the things he truly valued, and he didn't need some kid badmouthing him. Job or not, he'd be out of here, if that was the way Cade thought about him.

"If that's what you think of me, if you think you can't trust me, I'll call Dominic now and arrange for my replacement." Quinn pulled out his phone.

Cade's eyes went wide. "No. I didn't mean—"

"Do you want me to stay or not?" Quinn demanded.

"Yes."

No hesitation. Good. But Quinn was still angry.

"Go back to your rehearsal," he said and turned his back on Cade.

"Quinn, I—"

"Not now, Cade."

He walked away before either of them said something they'd regret.

In the kitchen he waited to see if Cade would follow him. There was nothing but silence, then footsteps away and the sound of the studio door opening and closing.

Quinn slumped against the kitchen counter. "Fuck," he muttered.

His fake boy was a jealous boy. This was going to be fun. Not.

He poured more coffee, sat on a stool at the bar, and scrolled through his phone contacts. He tapped the screen and waited to connect.

"Fuckoff."

Quinn grinned at the sleep-roughened voice. "Leo."

There was a long pause and Quinn wondered if Leo had gone back to sleep.

"Ryder?" Leo sounded more awake, if a little wary.

"Yeah."

"What are you doing calling at this hour?"

"I thought you'd still be awake."

"Early night," Leo said. "Got to bed about four."

"Sorry, I can call back."

Leo yawned in his ear. "'Wake now. What do you want?"

"Eric Strada."

"What about him?" Oh yeah, Leo definitely sounded wary now.

"What do you know about him?"

"Why?"

Quinn huffed, frustrated at the word play. "Don't play games, Leo."

"What's Strada to you?"

"Cade Connolly."

He heard a long exhale of breath, then Leo said, "Stay away from both of them."

"Why?"

"Because Strada still thinks the boy is his, and he won't give him up."

"You knew Strada was a psycho and you said nothing?"

Quinn said sharply. "What the fuck, Leo? You let a boy get hurt?"

Quinn couldn't believe what he was hearing. The community was small enough he'd been shocked that he'd not heard any rumors about Strada. Now to discover someone he knew and respected had known there was an issue and did nothing, said nothing...

"I didn't know he was hurting Connolly," Leo protested weakly. "I've only met the boy once. Total brat. I thought Strada had his hands full."

Quinn clenched his jaw. He couldn't say what he really thought without betraying Cade's trust and he wasn't going to do that.

"Have I fucked up?" Leo said.

"You have no idea," Quinn snapped and disconnected the call.

He stared into the murky depths of his coffee cup for long moments before his phone buzzed again. "Yeah?"

"I hear you've got an additional complication," Dominic said.

"Doug's a narc."

"Can you handle it?"

"Not sure," Quinn admitted honestly. "Depends on Cade."

"Let me know if you need to be reassigned."

One thing Quinn appreciated about Dominic was he was all business. "I will. Dominic, I need you to look into something for me before I make waves."

"Go on."

"Leo North. Owns a club in San Fran. I've known him for years. He's discreet. I called him to see if he knew about Strada."

"And?"

"He knew but he did nothing. Leo's not like that."

"You want me to find if there's any chatter?"

"Yeah. If I start asking questions it's only gonna cause problems."

"Will do," Dominic said. "And let me know if Connolly needs to be placed elsewhere."

Even the thought of Cade going to another bodyguard made Quinn feel sick, but he said curtly, "I'll let you know."

"Keep it together," Dominic snapped and disconnected the call.

Quinn growled. The bastard always had to have the last word.

Cade

The anger that flooded through Cade when he saw Quinn cuddling Ian was something he never expected. He felt like ripping Ian's throat out. How dare he cuddle Cade's Daddy.

Quinn is mine!

Except he wasn't, which made Cade angrier. And then he had to insinuate Quinn was into kids. His stupid mouth. He hated the look on Quinn's face. Like he'd disappointed him somehow. Quinn was angry and disappointed with him, and then he walked away. Cade felt like he was three years old.

He stomped back into the rehearsal. Ian shot him a worried look. So he fucking should. One word from Cade, and he'd be out.

"About fucking time," Keith bellowed, as oblivious as ever to the tension in the room.

Dave wasn't, though. He stared at both Ian and Cade like he was waiting for one of them—Cade—to explode.

"Cade—" Ian said.

"Later." Cade stalked over to his guitar and took a slow, deep breath. He had a job to do. He was a professional. Right?

* * *

"Get a fucking grip," Dave said bluntly at the end of three hours.

"What the fuck's wrong with you assholes?" Keith said.

The band was having a tense lunch in the kitchen.

Nothing had gone right from the start. Cade spent more time bitching at Ian than singing. After another failed start, Dave called it quits and they left the studio in search of coffee. Keith wanted beer, but Cade knew if he started drinking now they'd never get through the rehearsal.

Quinn wasn't in the kitchen, but there was a note saying to help themselves to the sandwiches and chips. Cade felt the anger burn through him again. This was his home, not Quinn's. He was the fucking host.

Keith descended on the food like a vulture. "You've gotta keep this boyfriend, Cade. He feeds us."

That was like a shock to Cade's system. Quinn was just playing a role. He was meant to be Cade's boyfriend, his Daddy. Of course he would feed his boy. Where the fuck was he?

"Cade," Ian said. "Can we talk?"

"For fuck's sake, whatever it is, kiss and make up," Keith mumbled, his mouth half full.

Maybe he wasn't so oblivious after all.

Cade stared coldly at Ian, but he nodded. "Come with me."

He led Ian into the den and turned to face him, his arms crossed.

Ian looked down at the floor and shuffled his feet. "I didn't know Quinn was your boyfriend. If I had, I'd never have hugged him. I swear."

"You have history."

"We played once or twice, that's all. Quinn has boys over for sessions sometimes."

Cade gritted his teeth. That piece of information wasn't helping. Ian caught Cade's eye and realized he must have said the wrong thing. Again. He held out his hands.

"What can I say to make this better, man? Quinn is a good guy, a good Daddy. He won't hurt you, unlike that other fucker."

"You really think he's a good Daddy?" Cade asked curiously.

"He's one of the best. He takes care of you whether it's for an hour or a year."

"Why hasn't he got a boy?"

Ian shrugged. "He's away a lot. Boys don't like that. I wanted someone who'd be around the whole time and he couldn't promise that."

"Have you got a Daddy?"

Ian hadn't mentioned it, but he was new to the band and Cade had been dealing with his own shit.

Ian's smile was tender. "I do. He's the best. He's there all the time."

"Do I know him?" The community was small enough, there was a good chance Cade would have met him.

"Graham Knight."

Cade blinked. "Wow."

"I know!"

Ian had the grandDaddy of the Daddies. Cade had been too nervous to talk to him the few times they'd met.

"You're very lucky," Cade said honestly.

Ian nodded. "I am. And I know it. But I'd never do anything to hurt you and Quinn. I want you to know that."

Cade let out a long sigh and knuckled his eyes. "I'm sorry for being a dick. I'm not as...certain as you are, and I let it get the better of me."

"He won't hurt you."

"That's what I thought about Strada," Cade said.

There was a long pause and then Ian said, "Have I still got a job?"

Cade felt like a total heel for upsetting Ian. "Yeah. You've still got a job. Come on. Let's get it right before Dave has an aneurysm."

Ian giggled. An outright giggle. "He's like an old mother hen, isn't he?"

"Ladies, have you kissed and made up?"

Cade rolled his eyes at Keith's bellow from the doorway. Their drummer had two volumes: outdoor and stadium. He turned to see Keith shoveling chips into his mouth. "Jeez, are you still eating?"

"Yup." Keith belched out the word for emphasis.

"Pig," Ian said with disgust.

Cade shook his head and grinned at Ian. "Let's get back to work before he cleans out my pantry."

He let Ian and Keith go ahead and took a moment to breathe.

"Are you all right?" Quinn asked from the doorway.

"No," Cade admitted, wrapping his arms around himself.

"What can I do to help?"

Quinn walked over to Cade and laid a hand on his shoulder.

"Could you hold me?" Cade saw the hesitation in Quinn's expression. "Just for a moment. I need to lean on someone." He felt like a pathetic piece of crap for asking, but he needed the comfort so bad.

Quinn tugged Cade in closer and wrapped his arms around him. Cade buried his face in Quinn's soft hoody. With his height and bulk it was almost smothering.

"It's like being hugged by a tree trunk," Cade muttered but he burrowed himself closer. He felt Quinn's chest leap under his cheek and realized the man was laughing.

"It's not the first time someone's said that to me," Quinn rumbled.

"Do you ever scare people?"

"Sometimes. I use my height and weight to advantage at work. Not normally with my boys, though."

Cade sighed and caught the lavender scent of detergent from Quinn's hoody. "Have you had a lot of boys?"

"Not of my own. Just boys who want the occasional session."

"Eric was my first."

"I'm sorry," Quinn said softly. He put his finger under Cade's jaw and forced him to look up. "You should never have been treated like that."

Cade could have drowned in Quinn's sympathetic gaze, but he hated the edge of pity. Cade didn't need pity. He'd let himself be manipulated and assaulted by Eric. He would never do it again. He'd never let anyone have that much power over him again.

Cade took a step back and Quinn let go of him. "I've got to rehearse."

"What time do you think you'll be done?"

"I don't know. It can go into the night sometimes."

Eric had hated that because it interfered with their social life. Eric liked to be seen with Cade.

Quinn nodded. "I'll make dinner for everyone."

"We usually order in."

"I'll make dinner," Quinn said implacably.

Cade opened his mouth to protest and shut it when he caught the glint in Quinn's expression. "Fine. Whatever."

Quinn frowned, obviously not liking the offhand dismissal. "Cade—"

But Cade hurried from the room. He needed to get away from Quinn's overpowering presence. It would be too easy to lay his head on Quinn's chest and beg him to hold Cade forever.

Chapter Seven

Quinn

Quinn was ready to throttle his client. "Absolutely not."

Cade faced off with him like a small angry duckling. If a duckling wore black leather, mascara and a pouty expression. "It's not your concern."

"Your safety is my concern and going out to a club after what happened last time is a stupid idea. You're not going clubbing," Quinn said.

The last thing he'd expected was the flat statement that Cade was going clubbing with the boys after rehearsal. He'd anticipated a quiet dinner and bed. But Cade had other plans. Some invite to a new club he'd forgotten about.

Cade scowled at him. "You're my bodyguard, not my Daddy. Guard me, pretend to be my Daddy, and keep your mouth shut."

Quinn folded his arms across his chest. Cade's eyes widened, but he didn't back down. "As your bodyguard I'm telling you it's a bad idea. Strada assaulted you last time. We've got no clue what he'll do this time."

Cade shrugged as if it were no big deal. "Last time I didn't have you with me. This time he'll leave me alone."

Quinn gritted his teeth. He wanted to shake some sense into Cade, but Cade wasn't the first client to ignore his advice, and he wouldn't be the last.

"Fine, but you follow my instructions at all times." He saw Cade narrow his eyes. "I mean it, Cade. The man wants to hurt you. If you're not going to listen to me, then you'd better find yourself another bodyguard. I won't work with clients who don't cooperate."

"You can't sack me. I'm the client."

"I can and I will. You don't cooperate and I walk."

"I'm taking my bike."

"Oh hell, no!" Quinn barked.

"I have to. I was given that bike as a sponsorship deal. I'm expected to show it off in public." Cade licked his lips, a nervous gesture Quinn found endearing. "You could ride with me and the team could follow us."

"You're think I'm gonna sit on the back?" Hadn't he noticed Quinn was the one in control?

"It's *my* Harley."

Quinn grunted. Yeah, he wouldn't let anyone else ride his, either. "I'll talk to the team."

"Whatever." Cade vanished back to the studio.

He was pushing and pushing and pushing. If he pushed Quinn too far, he wouldn't like the results.

Quinn picked up his phone. "Change of plan for the evening," he said when Tormac answered. "We're going clubbing."

"Okay, Jace is ready to follow when you are. Give us the club details and we'll have a team in place."

"Tell Jace he better fucking keep up," Quinn growled.

"On it."

Quinn disconnected and called Dominic.

"What?" CDR's operations manager sounded annoyed and distracted.

"You'd better get a replacement lined up."

"He's showing off. Deal with it."

"I'm not staying with clients who don't cooperate, and you told me I could walk away," Quinn said flatly.

"The situation's changed. Put him over your knee and spank him."

Then Dominic was gone and Quinn was left staring at the phone.

"Is this a do-over day?" he said to the empty room.

Then he realized he was about to go clubbing.

He made another call.

"What now?"

"I need to look like the biggest, baddest Daddy in the hottest club in town. What the fuck am I gonna wear?"

Dominic didn't stop fucking laughing.

* * *

Eleven pm and Quinn waited for Cade in the foyer. He was used to long days with clients, but it had been years since he went to a club outside the Daddy scene. He was in leather. Head to foot black leather with black biker boots. They talked about him wearing a designer suit, but he was a biker, not a damn fashion model. The leather was tighter than he'd usually have worn, and hugged his package. He knew he looked good when Cade came out of the den and stared at him, his mouth open.

"You're going like that?" Cade asked.

"Yeah."

"Wow."

Oh yeah, job done.

Cade was dressed in leather too, although less 'Daddy fuck me' style, and more 'look at me I'm the star'. His black shirt was so tight his nipple rings were clearly visible.

"Are you ready?" Quinn picked up his gloves and helmet.

"Yeah." Cade hastily dragged his eyes away from Quinn's groin. "I'm ready."

Quinn nodded. "I'm gonna alert the team here and at the club. Remember, you do what I say. If I tell you to duck, you hit the ground fast."

"This ain't my first rodeo, cowboy," Cade drawled. "You ain't my first bodyguard."

But I'm gonna be your last!

Whoa, where had that come from? Two weeks, remember? Just two weeks.

"We leave in five minutes," Quinn said before he said something he'd regret later.

"Okay." Cade seemed tired, less openly bratty than he was before.

"Do you still want to go out?"

Cade glowered at him. "Is this your way of telling me to stay home?"

Quinn shrugged. "I've got the team in place at the club, and Jace is ready to follow us. Whether we go or not is up to you."

Cade huffed and ran a hand through his hair. "The owner's a buddy of my manager. He promised him I'd turn up."

"Your manager arranges your social life?"

"With my PR team. I like clubbing. Everyone knows that."

Cade had a reputation for burning the candle at both ends. Strada had encouraged it. Made sure he and Cade were seen at the hottest places in town. Now Strada had lost his ticket to the VIP life. Quinn made a mental note to talk to CDR about that.

"Do you ever go to the Daddy clubs?"

Cade gave a quick shake of his head. "Eric said it wouldn't be good for my reputation. My contract has a morality clause. I'm 'allowed' to be gay within reason."

Interesting. Quinn added that to the list of things to discuss.

"Let's go," he said.

Jace waited outside with Cade's Harley. He rode a high-end Kawasaki. He was a sleek black guy who lived for racing his bikes. An injury had put him out of the pro-circuit, but he still followed it avidly. He and Quinn had been to many meets together. He smiled as they left the house. "Ryder, it's been a long time, man."

"Good to see you too," Quinn said, clasping his leather-clad hand.

He turned to see Cade glaring at him. Uh-oh, Cade was getting all possessive again. Jace had the sense not to say anything, just briefly smiling at Cade.

Cade swung onto the bike and Quinn crowded in close behind him and wrapped his arms around Cade's body.

"He's not a boy," Quinn said in Cade's ear.

"What?"

"He's not a boy. He's not in the scene at all. He's happily engaged to a lovely woman named Josie and they have a little girl called Lily."

"What the fuck do I need to know that for?" Cade muttered, but the tension eased from his muscles.

"Because I expect you to respect the guys watching your back."

Cade stiffened again but he said nothing as they rode out of the gates and headed downtown.

Quinn looked over his shoulder to see Jace on their tail. Jace gave him a thumbs up. He turned back to focus on the road ahead. He didn't like not being the one in control, but he had Cade in his arms. After a few minutes, Cade relaxed into his embrace. They looked like any couple out for a ride, and for a brief moment, Quinn wished it were true.

Cade

Cade faced forward, furious at himself as Quinn lectured him about respect. The muscle had no right to give him orders. He needed to be stronger than this. He should be the one giving orders, even if it went against every bone in his body.

He really had to get himself under control. He'd never been this possessive of boyfriends before, not even over Eric. Why did Quinn bring out the green-eyed monster in him? He wasn't in a relationship with Quinn, he was just there to guard his back.

Yet all Cade wanted to do was stay in Quinn's arms forever. And Quinn, *bastard*, knew that, or at least sensed it. Cade was just another boy to Quinn, in a long line of disposable boys. Cade gritted his teeth, angry at himself, angry at Quinn, and angry at Eric for treating him like Cade was nothing more than a hole in which to stick his dick.

"Hey."

Quinn's exclamation was almost lost in the rumble of

the Harley's engine, but his arms tightening around Cade jogged Cade from his dark thoughts.

"What?"

"Are you all right? You're shaking."

He was? Cade hadn't realized. Then he felt wet on his cheeks. Dammit, he'd been crying. He needed to concentrate on the road. The last thing he needed was to kill Quinn because he was upset at Eric.

"I'm okay." He yelled the lie loud enough for Quinn to hear.

Quinn said nothing, but he held Cade tight enough for Cade to draw strength from his embrace.

They reached the club without incident. Cade parked outside the front entrance. A line stretched down the block of people eager to get into the newest sensation in the club scene. Cade didn't have to wait in line. He was a VIP and there to be seen. Quinn got off the Harley and held his hand out to help Cade off the bike.

What the fuck?

Then Cade remembered this was all for show. Awkwardly he allowed Quinn to sweep him off the bike and set him on his feet on the sidewalk. There was an increase of chatter and then cries of recognition as he took off his helmet and shook out his hair.

"It's Cade Connolly."

"Who's tall, dark and dangerous with him?"

Cade wanted to snarl, "Mine," but then Quinn put his arm around Cade and the urge died away.

"We need to get inside," Quinn said.

Cade handed the key to Jace and allowed Quinn to guide him across the sidewalk and to the ropes. The doorman moved them aside and they entered the club, the street noise dying away as the door closed.

Tormac nodded at them as they were shown to the VIP floor and to their booth. The rest of the band was already there and, judging by the way Keith was listing to one side, already liquored up.

"Cade! Come here, baby!"

Keith went to wrap him in his usual sloppy hug, but Quinn tugged him back, flush against his body, a leather-clad arm tight across his chest.

Cade gasped and tilted his head, unsure why Quinn had suddenly gone caveman.

"I'm making it clear to whoever's looking you are mine, okay?" Quinn said, warm breath ghosting across Cade's ear.

"Okay," Cade breathed.

"He's yours, I get it. Now can I give him a hug?" Keith grumbled.

Quinn let Cade go and Keith gave him a half-hearted version of his usual hug. "Sorry," Cade murmured.

"Nah, it's cool. It's good to see you with someone who gives a shit."

The beer-soaked benediction was balm to Cade's soul. He just wished it were true.

Quinn slipped in beside him in the booth, their thighs jammed against each other. A waitress arrived to take their order. Cade wasn't surprised when Quinn stuck with water. He ordered soda as he wanted to ride his bike home. He needed to keep a clear head tonight. All of a sudden he felt tired and wished he'd stayed at home.

"They're gonna expect me to dance later," he said to Quinn. "I need to show myself."

His manager and PR team were always insisting he was visible. He wished sometimes he could say no.

"Okay." Quinn stood and held out his hand. "You want to dance?"

Cade blinked at him. "Now? With you?"

He'd expected to dance on his own or with the band. Eric had never wanted to dance with him.

Quinn rolled his eyes. "Do you want me to ask Ian?"

Cade felt the growl in the back of his throat. He was on his feet before he thought it through, his hand yanking Quinn toward the dance floor.

The smug expression on Quinn's face when he looked over his shoulder told Cade his green-eyed moment hadn't gone unnoticed. But by the time they reached the dance floor, Quinn led, and he reeled Cade into his arms. Cade ended up flush against Quinn's broad chest.

"Put your arms around my neck." Quinn bent to allow Cade to link his hands around Quinn's neck, then he held Cade against him, his hands on Cade's ass. "You only dance with me tonight, boy."

That 'boy' made Cade's heart sing even though he knew it was for show. But, being the brat he was, Cade tossed his head in challenge.

"Just you?"

"Just me. You don't have permission to dance with anyone else."

"Do you think you can keep up, old man?"

Cade reveled in the narrow-eyed glare Quinn gave him.

"Do you think I'm an old man?" Quinn demanded. He rolled his hips against Cade who couldn't miss the hardness against his lower belly. Cade shoved his hips against Quinn, letting Quinn know in no uncertain terms he was just as turned on. Christ, they must look as if they were trying to fuck each other on the dance floor.

The same thought must have occurred to Quinn because he eased back a fraction and bent his head. "Dance with me." His voice was a deep rumble that went through Cade's senses and made him shiver.

They danced, and Quinn did more than keep up. He led. And Cade followed willingly. At times men and women approached them, sometimes for Cade, just as often for Quinn, but Quinn declined all offers, making it clear they were exclusive. Cade knew this was all a show to hit the media. But Quinn treated him like they were the only two on the dance floor, and Cade let himself pretend, just for a moment.

They were both dripping in sweat. They drank bottles of water at the booth and returned to the dance floor. Cade stripped off his shirt and tucked it in Quinn's waistband. Quinn's eyes darkened as he studied Cade's smooth, shiny chest and the tiny rings in Cade's nipples. He licked his lips and God, didn't that make Cade harder still. He was going to come in his leather pants. He'd done that before. It wasn't pleasant.

The tempo slowed, and Quinn tugged him in closer. Cade rested his head against Quinn's chest, inhaling Quinn's musky scent. He closed his eyes and felt his Daddy hold him close. Just for now, he'd pretend.

Quinn said something, but Cade had been so lost in his thoughts, he missed it.

"What?"

"I need you to kiss me."

Cade raised his head. That...was an odd way to phrase it. "Kiss you?"

"Strada is here."

Panic went through Cade and he had to force himself not to wrench away from Quinn. "Where?"

"He's sitting at the booth next to ours. You're safe, Cade.

There are three men watching his every move. You're in my arms, and I'm between him and you."

Oh God! Oh God! Oh God!

"It's okay, Cade. I'm here to protect you."

Quinn's arms tightened around Cade, but his words made Cade feel like he'd thrown an icy bucket of water over him.

Protect him. Right. He was Cade's bodyguard, not his Daddy. This was all an act.

"Sure, you can kiss me," Cade muttered.

Quinn narrowed his eyes. "That's not what I said."

"Fine. I'll kiss you."

Cade reached up to give Quinn the briefest of kisses, but Quinn cupped a hand around Cade's neck and with the other hand cupped his ass, and kissed Cade as if he *owned* him. Cade felt a tear slip between his lashes. The kiss was so sweet and dominant at the same time. Quinn was telling the whole world that Cade was his, and Cade wanted so much for it to be true.

Quinn raised his head and looked down at him. He brushed away the tear with one finger. "Don't be frightened."

How could Cade tell him that at that moment he wasn't frightened of Eric? He was frightened of wanting more than Quinn could give him. He wanted the whole fairytale, not just this make-believe version.

"Boy."

Eric.

Cade shivered.

The fairytale had suddenly turned Grimm.

Chapter Eight

Quinn

Quinn spotted Strada as soon as he walked in. He'd been on high alert since they left the house, and he wasn't surprised to get the barked intel in his earpiece that Strada had just entered the premises. Strada strode through the club toward their booth, stopping short to talk to people in the next booth to them.

He didn't alert Cade, who rested his cheek against Quinn's chest as they danced. After what felt like hours of dancing, Cade seemed relaxed for the first time that day. Quinn held Cade close. He saw the exact moment Strada spotted Cade. The anger that flooded over his face was hard to miss. Quinn half-expected Strada to rip Cade out of his arms.

The team was in close proximity. Tormac closest with Jace, Ali, and Miles ready if they were needed. Quinn hoped to God Strada wasn't stupid enough to attempt to assault Cade again. He'd only escaped being locked up through the clever work of his lawyer. He wouldn't get away with it a second time.

When it looked as if Strada was about to make a move in their direction, he asked Cade to kiss him, repeating it when Cade didn't hear him. He knew he'd screwed up when Cade got angry, then terrified as he grasped Strada was here. Quinn had never intended for the kiss to be that intense, but he wanted Cade to focus on him and only him. Cade's mouth was everything he'd imagined it would be, warm, plump lips and a hot mouth he buried his tongue inside. He could just imagine sinking his cock inside the warm, wet channel. The tear on Cade's cheek when they pulled apart cut him to the quick. He wanted to wrap Cade up in his arms and hide him from the rest of the world.

The, "Boy," was as unwelcome as the panic on Cade's face.

Quinn dragged Cade into his arms before he had a chance to turn around. "Focus on me," he murmured. "You're my boy, not his. Mine."

Cade dragged in a shuddery breath and gave the briefest of nods. He turned his head to look at Strada. "Eric."

"We need to talk, boy."

Quinn eyed Strada coolly. The man was dressed in a designer suit, and Quinn was suddenly glad they'd decided against that for him this evening. His leathers were far more imposing.

"I'm not your boy. You need to stay away from me," Cade said coolly.

Only Quinn could feel him shake from fear. Quinn leaned against Cade, using his weight as a kind of comfort blanket.

"Cade—"

Quinn turned Cade so he was behind him and faced Strada. The man didn't blanch, but from the way his eyes narrowed, he was well aware of what Quinn was doing.

"You need to back off," Quinn said, his tone icy.

"I don't know who you are," Strada began.

"My name's Quinn Ryder." He knew from Strada's blink that he recognized Quinn. "Yeah, we've met. Now Cade told you to get lost."

"He's my—"

Before he could finish the sentence, Quinn leaned in so close he could smell the whiskey on the man's breath and see the tic under his right eye. "He's *my* boy now. Not yours. You lost that chance when you beat him up."

He didn't mention the rape, not wanting a member of the public to overhear, but the assault outside a club was on public record.

Strada tried to look around him. "Cade—"

Suddenly a balding man appeared with two guys larger than Quinn at his back. "Mr. Connolly, is there a problem here?"

Quinn gathered Cade close to him again. "Mr. Strada needs to leave."

Cade clung onto Quinn and nodded in agreement and the bald man, obviously part of the club security, turned to Strada. "Mr. Strada, please come with us."

The bald man made it clear who had the power in the room, and it wasn't the huge men or the daddies. Cade had the power, and he'd spoken.

Quinn waited to see what Strada would do. The primal part of him wanted a fight, wanted to be able to claim his boy publicly so that there was no doubt in anyone's mind who Cade belonged to. The protector part of him hoped

Strada was sufficiently intimidated by this show of civilized force to back the fuck off.

"Mr. Strada?" the bald man said, making it clear by his tone and his expression that he expected Strada to obey or he would be removed by force.

Strada huffed. "You can't keep avoiding me, boy," he said, and stalked toward the door, the three men following on his heels.

Cade shuddered, and Quinn tucked his head under his chin.

"It's okay, you're safe," he soothed.

The team melted to a safe distance. He nodded at Tormac, impressed by his decision to get club security involved. Now they would know for future that there was an issue. And Quinn had claimed Cade for his own.

Cade spoke but Quinn didn't hear him. He bent his head and asked for him to repeat it. Cade raised his head. "I want to go home."

"You sure?"

"I'm sure."

"Then we'll go. Give me a minute to make the arrangements."

He didn't know where Strada had gone, and he didn't want to risk him following them home, although it wasn't like Strada didn't know where Cade lived.

Quinn guided Cade back to the table. "Stay here," he said.

He heard Ian's worried, "Are you all right?" as he walked over to Tormac.

"We're leaving,"

"On it."

"Make sure we're not followed."

Tormac raised an eyebrow. "Anything else obvious you want to tell me?"

Quinn held back a snarl. "Just be careful." He caught Tormac's expression and sighed. "Too obvious?"

"Yeah." Tormac's frown deepened. "You know he's going to try again?"

"Now who's being obvious?" Quinn grinned at him, but it swiftly faded. "I do. He's obsessed with Cade and it's clear he'll do everything he can to get him back."

"If he's cornered he could be dangerous."

"Noted," Quinn said.

Tormac nodded. "Jace is ready. You're going out the back."

"Paparazzi?"

Quinn didn't put it past Strada to alert the paps and try to make a grand gesture in front of them.

"It's clear."

He returned to the booth, pleased to see Cade laughing at something Keith had said.

"We're ready to go," Quinn said to Cade.

Cade nodded and slid out of the booth.

"Aw, don't go yet. It's early," Keith protested, making a grab for Cade who evaded him.

"It's nearly three and I'm beat, man." Cade grinned down at his band mate. "I need my beauty sleep."

"Lightweight," Keith grumbled.

"Quit whining," Dave said. "I think I'm gonna call it a night too."

Keith sighed heavily and looked across at Ian. "It looks like it's just you and me, kid."

"Oh joy," Ian said, but he grinned at Keith.

Quinn ignored the by-play and looked at Cade. "We're going out the back."

Cade nodded. "What about my bike?"

"It's waiting for you. Don't worry, your baby is safe," Quinn teased.

They left, Quinn's arm around Cade. Quinn zipped up Cade's jacket over his naked chest as if he were a little boy. Cade's expression was conflicted, and Quinn understood.

"It's for show," he murmured. "You don't know whether Strada has friends here."

"He's got friends everywhere," Cade said, surprisingly, as Quinn put on his own jacket.

Quinn studied him. "That's a conversation we need to have."

"But not now." Cade sighed. "I just want my bed."

"It can wait until tomorrow."

He turned but Cade curled his fingers around his jacket. "Quinn."

Quinn looked down at him. "Yes?"

"I'm sorry." Cade bit his lip and Quinn wanted to free his poor abused lip from his teeth. "I should have listened to you. I didn't think Eric would be stupid enough to follow me here."

"How did he know you'd be here tonight?"

Cade looked troubled. "I said he had friends everywhere."

"Someone called him and told him you were coming." Quinn didn't like that idea.

"Anyone could have done that."

"In your band?"

Cade shook his head without hesitation. "No, Keith, Dave and Ian are loyal to me. Besides, they didn't like him."

Quinn thought he'd discuss that with each member of the band separately. But Cade was right. Anyone in the club could have called Strada.

"Why did he come?" Cade asked, his gaze locked on Quinn's.

"To check me out," Quinn said. He'd been thinking about that, too.

Strada hadn't made much of a scene. Hadn't started shouting or screaming. It had been a power-play. Testing Quinn, not Cade. What had Strada seen? Hopefully he'd realized Quinn was higher on the food chain than he was, and not to be pushed.

"He didn't like seeing me with you," Cade said.

"No, he didn't." Quinn took grim satisfaction from that.

Cade's lips twitched. "You know you're snarling."

He was? Quinn took a deep breath. He needed to keep himself under control. Especially around Strada. Quinn wanted him locked up, but by the book. It wouldn't be hard for Strada to wriggle free of any charges with a good lawyer. No, Quinn wanted him locked away for life. If that weren't possible, an eight to fifteen stretch would be good enough.

"Let's go home," Quinn said.

Cade nodded. "I need a cuddle with Mogs."

Quinn gave a loud snort. "You'll be lucky if she even acknowledges you exist."

Cade

Cade couldn't hold back his smirk.

"How the hell did you turn my cranky cat into a purring kitty?" Quinn shook his head at the sight of Mogs curled up on Cade's crossed legs as he sat on his bed.

"It's a gift," Cade said smugly.

Cats had always loved him. They'd arrived home to a scolding from Mogs for leaving her for so long. Cade had picked her up and crooned to her until she settled in his arms.

Quinn shook his head, grumbled under his breath, and said he was going to check the house to ensure everything was locked tight.

Cade grinned and went upstairs with the cat happily purring in his ear. He stopped in the doorway, realizing he hadn't noticed Quinn had made his bed before. He couldn't remember the last time he'd done it himself. Before Eric left maybe. Mogs chirruped, and he tried to ignore the misery threatening to settle in his gut. He needed a shower, but he needed Mogs's comforting presence more, so he settled on the bed, wearing just his leather pants, and paid her attention, scritching behind her ears until her eyes closed and she set up a steady rumble of happiness. He heard thumping footsteps up the stairs, then Quinn poked his head around the door.

"I'm going for a shower," Quinn said. "I'll be back in a moment."

Cade nodded. "I'll stay here with your cat." He was sure Quinn said something about traitors as he left the bedroom. Cade grinned at Mogs. "I think your Daddy is jealous," he crooned.

She closed her eyes again and purred even louder. Cade had a sudden fierce ache for the tiny kitten Eric had killed. Why had he taken something so precious? He had to blink back the sudden tears, or he'd be howling again. He felt as if he'd cried more for the kitten than for himself. Mogs pressed in close to him, as if sensing he needed comfort.

"You've got the best Daddy in the world," he whispered into her soft fur. He stayed where he was for a long time.

"That's better."

Quinn stood in the doorway, rubbing his hair with a

towel, wearing nothing but briefs, his package clearly outlined in the black cotton. Water droplets peppered his chest and down his tight abs. Cade wanted to lick up them all up again, and not stop licking until Quinn forgot his own name.

"Feel better?" he asked, forcing his mind away from those thoughts.

"Much. Do you want to shower?"

Cade wasn't sure if that was a question or an order, but either way it wasn't a bad idea. Apologizing to Mogs, he lifted her off his lap and into the nest she'd made on the pillows. He stood and stretched. His nipples hardened at Quinn's eyes on him. Then he caught a whiff of his armpit and grimaced. Yeah, he definitely needed a shower.

Quinn grinned at him. "Go wash up. We both need sleep."

"Where are you sleeping tonight?"

Quinn hesitated. "Where do you want me to sleep?"

Cade licked his lips. "In my bed."

"Okay. Go shower and I'll be here." No hesitation, no concern. Quinn headed to the bed and pulled back the comforter, dislodging Mogs once more, to her annoyance.

Relieved, Cade went into the bathroom and shimmied out of his leather pants. He stretched again and turned on the water, itching for the shower. The hot water was a blessing and he groaned as it pounded on his well-used muscles. It had been a while since he'd danced for so long. He closed his eyes, raised his face into the stream of hot water and let the heat and steam soothe him. Almost reluctantly, he focused on washing away the sweat, using his favorite shower gel with a hint of orange. He yawned, almost choked when he got a mouthful of water, and decided he needed to get out before he fell asleep in the shower.

Cade's eyes opened as he pushed open the stall door to see Quinn standing there with a towel. "Quinn. How long... I didn't know you were there."

Quinn snorted. "You were almost asleep. I was about to wake you up when you choked."

He started to dry Cade as if he were a small child. Cade stood there, a little embarrassed, getting a lot turned on, but if Quinn noticed Cade's stiffening cock, he didn't make any comment as he knelt to dry Cade's legs. He dried Cade's cock and balls with the same impersonal air, despite Cade's obvious interest.

"Come on. Bed." Quinn hung up the towel and led Cade to the huge bed, tucking him in as if he were a child, then moving around to the other side to climb in. He didn't switch off the light on the nightstand, evidently remembering Cade's fears from the night before. He settled, and Mogs circled a couple of times before delicately laying between them.

Cade stared up at the ceiling, his eyes prickling with sudden tears. He couldn't seem to quit crying at the moment. Quinn's kindness was undoing him. This big, gruff, Daddy bodyguard treated him with such tenderness he couldn't handle it. He was used to getting shouted at, instead he got soft touches and gentle words. Cade had no fucking idea how to handle that.

"Come here, boy." Quinn scooped Mogs out of the way, and tugged Cade gently. Too tired to argue, Cade rolled over into Quinn's chest and any chance of not crying vanished. Quinn held Cade tight and he wept until he'd cried himself out again.

"Getting to be a habit," he mumbled, when the shuddering sobs had subsided, and he was left wrung out.

Quinn stroked his hair. "It's not a problem."

Cade believed him and stayed where he was. He was too tired to be bratty and brave by himself. He wanted to be protected from the world. He wanted Quinn to hold him until he fell asleep, then shelter him for the rest of the night. Quinn ran his hand down Cade's back, tracing soothing circles.

"No one's ever held me just to comfort me," Cade said.

"It's one of the things I enjoy the most about taking care of a boy."

A boy, not *his* boy.

"What do you do in the sessions you have with boys like Ian?"

Quinn took his time and, for a moment, Cade thought he wasn't going to get an answer.

"I give them what they need for the session. Some are high-powered men who just like to hand over the responsibility of being an adult to me. I feed them, soothe them, read stories to them. Others want to be littles. Some boys ask me to discipline them in a way they can't have in real life."

Cade processed that. "What do you get out of it?"

"I'm a nurturer. I like taking care of men."

"Protecting them," Cade offered.

Quinn hummed above his head. "Yes."

"Is that why they asked you to be my... bodyguard?"

"I think so. Someone wanted to show you what it's like to be taken care of."

"I've never had that. I was a foster kid and then I met Eric. He trained me to take care of him." He felt Quinn tense above him. "It was my fault. I didn't do any research."

"It wasn't your fault," Quinn insisted. "Strada should have cherished you, not abused you."

Cade sighed. "I just thought all Daddies were like him. I wish I'd known what I was getting into."

"Me too, little one, me too."

Cade's eyes fluttered shut, sleepiness overtaking him, and he sank into the feel of Quinn wrapped around him. He sensed, rather than felt, Quinn press a kiss into the top of his head.

Almost asleep, he wasn't sure if he heard Quinn whisper or if he dreamed it. "You deserve so much better than him, Cade. I wish you'd let me show you that."

Then he was asleep and there were no nightmares. Just warmth and safety and protection. Because Quinn didn't let him go.

Chapter Nine

Quinn

Quinn woke up feeling as if he were being slowly crushed. He cracked open one eye to find Cade almost on top of him, still holding him tight. Quinn would bet Cade hadn't let go of him all night. For a little guy, Cade was heavy. Quinn rolled them both onto their sides and took a deep breath, much to the relief of his lungs.

Last night had been hard work all around for them. Quinn hadn't wanted to go to the club, and seeing Strada there had added to his misgivings. He was just grateful Strada hadn't caused too much of a scene.

Quinn didn't want to say, "I told you so," to Cade, but maybe now Cade would listen to him. Strada wasn't going to give up without a fight. At least now Strada had seen them together, and Quinn had made his claim. Would that make Strada escalate or would he back down? Quinn had a feeling Strada wasn't the type to back the fuck off.

He raised his head to take a look at the clock and

blinked. Eleven. He never slept that late, although it had been nearly five before they settled down to sleep. Cade's whispered confessions still rattled around in his head. He'd never met a boy who needed so much nurturing. Would Quinn be strong enough to walk away at the end of two weeks?

Cade grumbled under his breath and pressed in closer. The boy liked his Quinn-blankie.

"Good morning," Quinn murmured.

Cade smacked his mouth a couple of times and opened his eyes, staring straight into Quinn's. "Hey." His voice sounded rusty.

Quinn lay on the pillows, one large hand on Cade's hip. "Did you sleep?"

"I did. No nightmares. I feel like shite though. What time is it?"

"Eleven. We slept through."

Cade groaned. "I think I missed a meeting with my PR guys."

"It's okay," Quinn said. "I'll text Dominic. He can rearrange it for you."

Dominic was going to be so pleased to act as Cade's social secretary.

"Thanks." Cade yawned. "Sorry. I feel like I could sleep for a million years."

"You need to eat."

"I don't—"

"You need to eat," Quinn repeated as he got out of bed.

Cade grumbled but he sat up, rolling his shoulders and scratching his belly. Quinn appreciated the sight of his broad shoulders and lean muscles. He wanted to lean forward and lick each freckle on his shoulders.

"You know I'm a grown up, yeah?" Cade pointed out. "I can make these decisions for myself."

Quinn ignored him. "I'll see you downstairs for brunch."

He grinned at Cade's scowl as he left the bedroom. Mogs followed Quinn, probably in the hope of a very late breakfast.

"So much for loyalty, kitty-kat," Cade muttered.

Quinn's grin turned into a broad smile. Then his stomach rumbled. He definitely needed food.

He went into the guest bedroom and shrugged on a hoody and sweats, before going downstairs. Mogs yelled at him impatiently until he filled her bowl, then she retreated to the corner with an aggrieved huff to eat her breakfast.

Coffee next. He knew that was going to be the first thing Cade would look for when he came downstairs.

As Quinn waited for the coffee to drip through, he received a phone call. He frowned as he saw the caller ID. Leo North. What did he want?

"Leo," he said coldly.

"I know you're pissed with me," Leo said.

Quinn blinked. Okay, so starting on the offensive. "Yes."

"Let me explain."

"Okay." Quinn wasn't going to give an inch. He listened out for Cade coming downstairs but there was silence.

"I was shocked at your accusation," Leo said.

"Shocked? Or annoyed?"

"Both," Leo admitted honestly. "It's hard to hear someone I thought a friend being called an abuser."

Unseen by Leo, Quinn nodded. He could understand that. It didn't excuse Leo though. "So why're you calling me?"

"I did some digging. Cade isn't the first."

"No shit, Sherlock."

"Do you want to be pissy or do you want to listen?"

"I'm listening," Quinn growled.

Leo huffed. "I talked to some of his previous boys. They were reluctant to talk until I assured them it wouldn't get back to Eric."

"They were afraid of the repercussions."

"Yes."

"So how many has he abused?"

Another long sigh from Leo. "At least four that I know of."

"What the hell?" Quinn exploded. "Four of your boys abused and no one does anything?"

"How could we do something when we didn't know? As far as I knew they just dropped out of the scene. I had no idea he'd…"

"Raped them," Quinn supplied.

"Yes." Leo sounded as if he'd aged a million years.

"What are you going to do?"

"I've told each boy if they want me to go to the cops with them, I'll do that. None of them are keen on the publicity."

Quinn grunted. Hardly surprising. "What else?"

"Eric is banned from any participation in the lifestyle here. No clubs will accept him. Everyone is gutted. The boys are coming in to talk to me tomorrow as a group. They were reluctant at first, until I told them they weren't alone."

"Have you mentioned Cade to anyone?"

"No. I said I'd been approached anonymously."

"Good. You keep Cade's name out of this, understand? If this gets out, Cade's whole life implodes."

"I get it, Ryder. This ain't my first rodeo."

Quinn grimaced. He knew Leo was doing his best to

make up for yesterday, but his trust in the man had taken a serious knock.

"Has anyone contacted Eric?" he asked.

"No. Eric hasn't been back here for months."

"Okay, if we can keep it that way, I'd be grateful. He's coming after Cade. I don't want his attention diverted."

"You want him to come after your boy?" Leo sounded shocked.

Quinn was about to say Cade wasn't his boy when he remembered to the outside world Cade was very much his. "I need him to make his move. Then I'm going to gut him."

Leo was quiet for so long Quinn wondered if they'd been disconnected. "I thought he was my friend."

"And now?"

"I'll never forgive him for hurting boys in his care."

Quinn nodded again unseen. That was the reaction he'd expected yesterday. "You take care of those boys. If they need anything, you let me know."

"We can take care of our own." Leo sounded offended.

Except you didn't. You left them hanging out to be abused.

But he didn't push it, merely saying, "Just let me know, yeah?"

"I will." Another long pause. "Tell Cade I'm sorry."

Quinn wasn't going to tell Cade a damn thing. Cade was his to deal with. "Bye."

Leo said goodbye and disconnected. Quinn thought for a moment: then, since there was still no sound from Cade, he called Dominic.

"What now?"

"There's at least another four boys that I know of who've been abused by Strada."

"There's bound to be more," Dominic said.

Quinn agreed. "If we can get someone to come forward publicly, then hopefully it will be like dominos falling."

"If Cade—"

"You know that isn't going to happen," Quinn said.

"I know. In the meantime, what the hell were you thinking letting him go to the club last night?"

Quinn had been waiting for Dominic to yell at him. "He's strong-willed."

"You're supposed to be the Daddy."

"Fake Daddy," Quinn reminded him. "And therein lies the problem. Cade doesn't want a Daddy."

"Of course he does," Dominic said. "He just doesn't trust you yet."

It never ceased to amaze Quinn that Dominic was very straight and married with a kid, yet he talked about gay kink as if he were part of the scene.

"He needs to go into a safe house," Dominic said.

Quinn winced. "He won't agree."

"Then make him agree," Dominic snapped. "We can't afford for this to go tits up."

Tits up?

Dominic continued. "We'll get Strada off the streets."

"That's your job. Mine is to protect Cade."

"Bollocks," Dominic barked. "You want to be the one to take him down."

"Bollocks? Tits up? What the hell are you talking about?"

"I've been around the Brits too long," Dominic muttered. "And don't deflect."

Dammit, Dominic knew him too well. "I want to see him rot in hell, but I'm not going to let him hurt Cade."

"Then put him in a safe house."

"What's happened?" Cade said.

"I've got to go," Quinn said to Dominic and disconnected the call before Dominic could continue shouting at him. He turned to smile at Cade. "Just catching up with CDR. Ready to eat?"

Cade

Cade listened to Quinn go down the stairs and smirked into the sheet.

Sucker!

He grabbed Quinn's pillow to hug, and closed his eyes with a happy sigh. He had no intention of getting out of bed. Adult here. Cade didn't need to be tied to Quinn's schedule. He'd go back to sleep and wake up at a normal hour like four.

He heard Quinn in the kitchen and his stomach rumbled loudly.

"You can shut up too."

Another loud rumble.

Cade flopped onto his back. Maybe the universe was telling him he needed to get off his butt and go find coffee. That was all he needed. Coffee, and then he'd come back to bed. Cade pushed back the covers and looked down at himself. He was naked. He hadn't even realized he'd gone to bed without wearing pajama bottoms or sleep shorts. Quinn had dried him and put him to bed as if he were a small child. Cade felt his cheeks heat. He'd felt wanted and cared for and protected. Would it be too much to ask for that?

His belly growled again.

"Okay, okay, I get the picture."

Cade shoved on a pair of sweats lying in the corner and an old T-shirt with a faded picture of David Bowie, and went in search of coffee.

He could smell the Java as he ran down the stairs and heard Quinn talking to someone.

Quinn sounded grim. "I want to see him rot in hell, but I'm not going to let him hurt Cade."

"What's happened?" Cade said.

"I've got to go," Quinn said, turning to smile at Cade as he disconnected the call. "Just catching up with CDR. Ready to eat?"

Cade narrowed his eyes. He wasn't stupid. He knew Quinn was hiding something.

"Sit down," Quinn said, "Perfect timing. I'm just about to make an omelet."

Cade glowed under the praise, then he glowered. "I just need coffee."

"And food. Don't argue."

Cade opened his mouth to do just that, but Quinn steered him to the stool and before he knew what he was doing, he had coffee in a large mug and Quinn was beating eggs.

Within a couple of minutes, Quinn placed a light and fluffy omelet in front of him.

Cade opened his mouth to say he wasn't hungry, but Quinn popped a forkful of omelet in his mouth.

"Good?" Quinn asked.

Cade chewed and swallowed. "The best. But I only need—"

"If you say coffee one more time, I'm going to cuff your wrists behind your back and feed you myself."

Quinn's face was serious. Cade wanted to tell him to get lost, but Cade's traitorous dick thought the idea of being cuffed and fed was more than hot.

"Someone likes the idea," Quinn rumbled.

"Yeah, well, I'm not gonna listen to my dick."

"Shame." Quinn handed him the fork. "Are you gonna feed yourself?"

"If you give me more coffee."

"Deal."

Cade was halfway through the omelet when he looked over to Quinn who was eating the same thing. "Is it always gonna be like this?"

Quinn shook his head. "Sometimes you're going to have to obey me without question."

Cade wanted to make a crack, but he realized Quinn was deadly serious. "I'll do it," he promised.

Quinn gave him a wry smile. "Then I'll accept the odd bratty behavior."

"I'm always gonna be a brat," Cade said.

"You're only a brat because you're always trying to test your boundaries."

Cade carried on eating for a while. "Eric was strict," he said eventually.

"Strada was abusive."

"Sometimes it's the same thing." Daddies had to punish their boys. That's what Eric had told him.

Quinn shook his head, his expression grim, yet pitying. Cade resented being pitied.

"It's not. I hope you find the Daddy who can show you that."

"I don't need a Daddy."

It sounded more and more like a lie in Cade's head.

* * *

"What are your plans for the rest of the day?" Quinn asked as they finished up the toast.

Cade sighed. "I should talk to my management

company and PR guys. They need to know about Eric. Then I need to touch base with Louis, who's organizing the entertainment for the event."

"Louis Romero?"

"You know him?"

Quinn hesitated. "We've met."

Cade took a moment, then it fell into place. "He's a Daddy?"

Louis was a tall, handsome guy in his late thirties. He ran one of the most successful entertainment businesses in Seattle. He was a calm, organized, go-to guy. Whatever you needed, he would provide it. Cade's band had been on his schedule of entertainers for years. Cade could imagine him as a Daddy.

"Not exactly," Quinn murmured.

Cade blinked at him. "Really? But he's, like, one of the top men in Seattle."

He'd always felt small in Louis's presence, even though the man was never anything but nice to him.

Quinn looked at him over the rim of his mug. "I told you some of the men who see me are high-powered."

"Wow."

"It's not general knowledge."

"I understand." Cade cocked his head. "You're well-known on the scene."

"I am."

"Why did no one know about Eric? Why did no one warn me?"

He saw anger and frustration in Quinn's eyes.

"I've been trying to find that out myself," Quinn growled. "There's gonna be a lot of hard questions asked."

"Were there others?"

"Yes."

At least Quinn didn't try to hide it.

"Here?"

"I don't know. I know of others in San Francisco."

Cade looked down at the table. "I probably know who they are."

"You know Daddy Leo?" At Cade's nod, Quinn said, "He's handling it. Don't worry."

"One of them tried to tell me but I wouldn't listen. I was so proud of Eric wanting me."

"Don't blame yourself, Cade. Eric is charismatic and, I imagine, an excellent manipulator. I met him once. I had no idea he abused his boys."

Cade couldn't help feeling he could have done something.

"Stop." Quinn laid a hand over Cade's. It felt warm and protective. "You are not at fault here."

"It's hard not to blame myself." Cade tugged his hand away and wrapped his arms around himself.

"Cade."

Cade looked away from Quinn.

"Cade, look at me."

It was an order. He could hear it in the tone and inflection. Quinn expected to be obeyed. Quinn would hurt him if he disobeyed. Cade closed his eyes. Remembered the pain. He couldn't obey. Not now. Panic shot through him. He couldn't breathe. He rocked backward and forward, his lungs burning.

Then hard arms wrapped around him, and he was held firm in Quinn's arms. He gasped.

"Breathe in," Quinn said in his ear. "Now breathe out. Breathe in, breathe out."

He repeated it over and over, his warm breath ghosting

over Cade's ear. It took Cade a long time before he could focus on Quinn's words.

He gasped again.

"Good. Breathe in. Breathe out."

Quinn kept repeating it, slowly and calmly, like there was nothing odd about a man having a panic attack in his arms. Cade focused on the rhythmic quality of his voice until breathing was automatic and no longer a struggle.

"Dammit." Cade pulled away. "I've got to get myself under control."

Quinn stroked Cade's head. "Give yourself a break, boy. You've got the biggest event of your life coming up, an asshole trying to lure you back to the dark side, and an international trip. It's no wonder you're stressed."

It sounded good, Quinn calling him boy, but it was just an affectionate term. It had no meaning. He pulled back and huffed. "More coffee?"

"Coming up," Quinn agreed. He cupped Cade's jaw and looked into his eyes. "I'm here for you."

"I know. Thank you." He leaned into Quinn's hand.

"Go make your calls," Quinn said.

Cade nodded. "I think I'll take the Hog out later."

Quinn's expression darkened. "No."

"No?" Cade shook off Quinn's hand. "You don't get to tell me what to do."

"Shut up, Cade. Of course I fucking tell you what to do. It's my job."

And then Quinn walked away. Just fucking walked away, leaving Cade staring after him.

Chapter Ten

Quinn

Quinn took a grim satisfaction in walking away from Cade. It was that or spank him. At some point Cade was going to have to realize that, when it came to his personal protection, Quinn was top dog, alpha boss etc. Of course, Quinn insisted on being alpha boss in any situation, which was why he generally worked with small teams, and on his own where he could. He was lucky that most of the time CDR gave him his head.

He retreated to the den to catch up on conversations with the team who would be handling security at the live event. Big gigs were always a nightmare, with so much potential to go wrong.

"You know I'm managing the bike event, don't you?" Griff Larson groused as Quinn ran through his list of questions... okay, orders.

"Yes."

"You could sound more convincing."

"My client is challenging."

"I'd heard," Griff said dryly. Griff understood this was code for Cade would be a pain in the ass if he got the opportunity.

"If he can find a way to buck the system, he will."

"It's all cool, Ryder, he's not the first client to need careful handling and he sure as hell won't be the last."

Quinn breathed easier. Larson and his team had a reputation for solid work, which was why he'd asked for them.

"Don't let him run circles around you," Quinn said.

Griff gave a long throaty chuckle. "I'll put the boy over my knee if he gives me any trouble."

Quinn bristled. No one but him was going to lay a hand on Cade.

Griff's chuckle turned into a belly laugh. "You know you're growling."

"Fuck you," Quinn snapped, but he had a smile curving his lips. Griff was an old friend of his and knew how to push his buttons.

"You've gotten very possessive in a short time."

"I haven't."

"Liar," The humor had disappeared out of Griff's voice. "Ryder, is there something you need to tell me?"

"No." Then a firmer, "No."

Griff hummed, obviously not believing him. "Okay. Well, you know where I am if you need to talk it out."

The last thing Quinn needed was a lecture, but then the anger drained away as he realized he was being an ass. Griff had been a friend and coworker for a long time. "I do. Thanks for having my back."

"Always. Now fuck off," Griff said. "I've got an event to plan."

"Yeah, yeah. Thanks—"

But Quinn was talking to empty air, as Griff had discon-nected the call.

"Love you too, asshole."

He felt more relieved about security plans, though. Griff had anticipated most of his questions and had a few more of his own.

Next he placed a call to London.

"QuickFire Securities. How may I help you?"

"Is Liam Quick available?"

"Let me check. Who shall I tell him is calling?"

"Quinn Ryder from CDR."

While he listened to some godawful music, Mogs came in and sat on his lap, demanding his attention. He obliged, caressing her until she was a furry puddle of purrs.

"Quick. Is there a problem with Connolly, Ryder?"

So, no small talk then. Quinn could work with that.

"Nothing I can't handle," Quinn assured him. "I'm calling about Strada."

"He didn't come to London. I believe he doesn't like traveling."

"I heard that too. Were you alerted to any potential threat while Cade was there?"

"You mean did Strada hire someone to hurt Connolly?"

"Or stalk him. Make sure he didn't step out of line."

"My team weren't aware of any pros. There were the usual over-enthusiastic fans who had to be discouraged. You know what some of the women are like."

Quinn grunted in agreement. He certainly did. He'd had to wrestle with more than one uber-fan, desperate to get near their idol. "And guys?"

"No one that stood out. Do you have anyone in mind?"

"No. Just covering all bases."

"I don't have the team notes, as the band hired my

previous company, but I'll contact the team members to see if they remember anything."

"That would be great. Thanks, Liam."

There was a hesitation. "How are you getting on?"

Quinn's lips twitched. "We're doing fine. He's behaving."

"Good." Quick's relief was almost comical.

Quinn ended the call on a chuckle. He was deep into scheduling the next few days when Doug called.

"Yup?"

"Your client's left the building."

So much for behaving.

Quinn sat bolt upright, dislodging Mogs who fell off his lap with an indignant yowl. "Who's with him?"

"Padraig. I had a feeling you didn't know."

"On wheels?"

"Yeah. He seems to be heading for the beach. Jace will meet you there too."

Quinn wasn't surprised at the destination. He knew Cade spent a lot of time by the sea to get inspiration. He'd seen many interviews where he'd said listening to waves fed his soul. Whatever that meant.

"I'm on my way," he barked into the phone.

He cursed as he wriggled into his leather jacket and gloves and stomped into his boots. He grabbed his helmet and bolted for the door. He was going to put Cade over his knee and spank his ass until it was red.

But first he had to catch him.

"What the hell do you think you're doing?" he said out loud to the empty house. Then he sprinted around to the garage, not surprised to see Doug waiting for him.

"Padraig has him in sight. He's changed destination.

Head for the Japanese Garden," Doug said, handing him an earpiece.

"Padraig?"

"I'm here." The soft Irish-American accent was barely audible above the engine and road noise.

"The tracker is working well," Doug said.

Quinn and the CDR team weren't born yesterday. They knew Cade was likely to bolt at some point. The tracker had been installed on the bike before it was returned to Cade.

"Okay. I'm gone," Quinn said, as he gunned the engine. His Hog was built more for reliability than speed, but she'd get him there.

The gates opened as he approached, and one of Doug's team waved at him while he concentrated on a phone call. Quinn knew Dominic would have already been informed.

Cold anger coursed through him as he negotiated the busy streets. Defying him was a stupid, stupid thing to do. He had said no, and he expected to be obeyed, not to have to fight Cade on every corner.

Quinn had to face up to a hard truth. If Cade defied him over his safety, he couldn't work with him. It was one thing to go to a club with a full team of security, but to go out on his own without arranging with Quinn first—that was putting himself deliberately in danger. Despite all appearances to the contrary, Cade wasn't stupid. He knew Eric was escalating. So why had he done this?

"Doug?"

"Here."

"Get CDR to check Connolly's phone. I want to know if something prompted his flight."

"On it."

"Quinn?" Padraig cut in.

"Here," Quinn said.

"Get to the Japanese Garden as quick as you can."

Tension flooded through Quinn and he had to take a deep breath before he could answer. "Strada?"

"I think so. He's at a distance, but I'm sure that's him. Connolly seems oblivious to him at the moment."

"Doug," Quinn said.

"Got it. Dominic wants to keep this low-key."

Quinn ground his teeth. "If Strada makes a move on Cade, I'm going to shoot him."

"Negative. You're there to play the jealous boyfriend and protect Cade. Padraig will take down Strada."

In your dreams!

"Quinn?" Doug said sharply.

"I heard."

He quit talking then, and focused on getting to the garden as fast as possible without killing a passerby or himself. Why had Cade gone there instead of the beach? Was it to confuse the team?

Quinn arrived at the Japanese Garden to see Padraig in the parking lot. Quinn parked his bike by Cade's and joined Padraig.

"Where the hell is Cade? Why aren't you with him?"

"Jace followed Strada in. At the moment they're sitting on a bench, talking. I'm your backup."

Padraig handed Quinn a ticket. "Go get your boy."

Quinn rolled his eyes. He followed Padraig through the garden. Quinn had been to the Japanese Garden before and it was stunning, but today he barely noticed, intent on reaching Cade.

"There." Padraig nodded in front of him. "By the lake."

Quinn's worst nightmare was realized as he took in the

sight of Cade and Strada deep in conversation. He couldn't see their expressions, but they looked relaxed enough.

"Quinn," Doug said in his ear. "Cade received a call from Strada just before he left."

"Got it," Quinn bit out.

Another hard truth. Maybe Strada's sick brand of Daddyhood was what Cade wanted. No, Cade didn't know any different. Whether he wanted Quinn or not, he had to be made to see that Strada was a toxic mess. Quinn had told him about the other boys. Why the hell did he agree to meet him?

"You need to get over there," Padraig said.

Quinn started, lost in his thoughts. What the hell? He'd allowed himself to become distracted, to moon over the fact Cade didn't want him, while his client was standing next to the fucking bad guy. Jeez, he should be fired right now.

"Going," he muttered.

"Don't get between me and Strada," Padraig cautioned.

"Got it."

Quinn rolled his eyes as he strode over the grass to the bench. *I know that, thanks, Dad!*

Neither Cade, nor Strada, saw Quinn approach. It gave Quinn a chance to assess them, and he quickly realized one thing. No matter the smile on Cade's face, it did not reach his eyes. He was terrified. Strada, on the other hand, was relaxed, a warm smile on his face, talking like nothing had ever happened between them, like he hadn't raped his boy. Just the thought made Quinn want to shoot him where he sat. No, he had to play this right. He was the Daddy, so first he had to get his boy in check.

"Boy!" he bellowed.

Cade

Meeting Eric had been a stupid idea, but Cade had been desperate to get out of the house, and Quinn saying no to him riding his bike and then just walking off made him seethe. He just wanted an hour away from the house. Was that too frigging much to ask for? And then Quinn walked away. Like he was nothing.

Yeah, it had been stupid, especially after last night. He knew Eric couldn't accept they were over. He'd gotten Eric's call at the exact moment he wondered how he could piss off Quinn. Cade knew Eric still had things of his at his house. He'd written them off. But now Eric offered to bring them to the garden. A chance for them to talk in one of Eric's favorite places, and for him to get his belongings. He'd blown past security, guilty and ecstatic. Even if Padraig or Jace was there, they wouldn't be able to catch up with him.

But the moment he saw the look in Eric's eyes, he knew he'd been foolish. Eric didn't want to talk, and he didn't have Cade's possessions. What he wanted was to hurt Cade.

"Boy."

Cade closed his eyes. Oh, thank God—Quinn was here.

Cade turned, seeing the myriad of emotions in Quinn's expressive eyes. Yes, anger. But relief too. The relief at finding Cade was obvious. But also possessiveness. If Quinn was faking his possessiveness, he was doing a good job.

Strada, however, was not relieved. He was furious. Good.

Quinn stopped, planted his boots firmly on the grass, folded his arms across his chest, and fixed his gaze on Cade.

"Boy, come here."

Without hesitation, Cade stumbled over to Quinn and allowed him to gather his slender body against Quinn's broad chest. He felt a knot of tension ease as Quinn wrapped him in his arms. Tremors ran through him, and Quinn tightened his grip.

"Sometimes you're going to have to obey me without question."

This was one of those times.

After I screwed up, bigtime.

Yeah, after that. He'd be lucky if Quinn ever spoke to him again.

Strada glowered at Quinn. "What are you doing here? This is a private conversation."

"Which you're having with *my* boy without *my* permission," Quinn said coolly.

Cade trembled again. Quinn leaned into him and Cade rested his head against Quinn's chest. Quinn laid his cheek on top of Cade's head. Strada's eyes narrowed at the intimate gesture. Cade wasn't surprised when Strada went on the offensive.

"He's not your boy. I know who you are, and I know what you do. You're a bodyguard. Muscle."

Dammit, Strada had discovered their act this early. Was it his fault?

Then Strada sneered at Quinn. "All brawn and no brain. He won't want you. He needs someone who can control him."

Wait! A lightbulb went on. Strada knew who Quinn was. Did he think Quinn wasn't good enough for Cade? No fucking way!

"Like you controlled me, Eric? With your fists? With your dick? Like you controlled me with blood and pain?" He trembled so hard Quinn almost lost his grip.

Strada's expression hardened. "You're a brat. You needed to be punished."

"You don't punish boys by abusing them," Quinn snapped. "Cade was new to this. He needed love and kindness."

"Look where that got you," Strada said. "He would never have run off to speak to another man when he was with me."

That stung more than it should have.

"I only came because you said you had some of my things." Cade licked his lips. "I knew you were busy...Daddy."

They both held their breath at the honorific.

Quinn raised Cade's chin to force him to look into his eyes. "Strada has a point. Next time you tell me. I didn't like finding out with a note."

Cade's eyes narrowed: there'd been no note, but he quickly cottoned on. "I'm sorry, Daddy."

Quinn bent and kissed him deeply, claiming him so Strada could have no doubt who owned Cade now. It was like before. Cade's brain switched off, his whole focus on Quinn's mouth.

Quinn raised his head. Cade whimpered at the loss of his mouth. But Quinn's attention was on Strada. "I thought I made it clear in the bar. Stay away from Cade. Don't call him, don't 'accidentally' bump into him, and don't send him fucking flowers."

Strada narrowed his eyes. "What are you talking about?"

"Flowers. Don't send them. Ever. Leave Cade alone."

"I haven't sent him flowers."

"Yes, you did," Cade said. "You sent me black roses, two days ago."

Eric shook his head. "I wouldn't send you black roses.

You know I hate roses. I don't know what you're talking about."

"You're lying," Cade said.

"I'm not," Strada insisted.

Much as Cade hated the idea, he believed Eric. Suddenly his blood ran icy-cold. If Strada hadn't sent them, who had?

He tilted his head up to look at Quinn. "Does this mean—?"

"We'll talk about this later," Quinn said. "Let's go home."

He guided Cade away from Eric without another word.

"He's not yours," Eric yelled after them.

"Which one of us is he talking to?" Cade muttered.

"Does it matter?" Quinn asked.

Cade thought about it for a moment. "No, not really." He looked up to see Jace and Padraig waiting for them. "Were they here the whole time?"

"Yes. Padraig followed you."

Cade sighed. "I wish I'd known. I might not have felt so alone and scared."

Quinn tightened his arm around Cade. "You know we're going to have to talk about this."

"I was an idiot," Cade admitted.

"Yes."

"You know I'm a celebrity, right? Most people wouldn't let me call myself an idiot."

"It's not my job to tell you what you want to hear," Quinn said. "Get yourself a personal assistant if you want a lapdog. It's my job to keep you alive."

"I believed Eric when he said he didn't send the flowers." There was a long pause and Cade looked up to see the troubled look on Quinn's face. "You do too?"

"Yes," Quinn admitted. "I think he'd brag about it, not deny it."

"That means…"

"That means we do our homework and find out who sent you the flowers."

Cade shivered. "How many crazy people are out there?"

"Too many to count, boy, but we're just concerned with the ones who are interested in you."

"Talk to my manager. She keeps all the letters and informs the police of any of the extra nutty ones."

"I'll do that. It was on my list to liaise with your management company and PR firm today. The day's kinda run away from me."

Cade looked up at him. "I'm sorry."

Quinn's expression was stern but tender. It was an intriguing combination. Cade wanted to run his fingers over Quinn's mouth and cheeks and nose. To learn him.

"Cade?"

Cade blinked, then felt his cheeks heat. He'd been so lost in staring at Quinn he'd forgotten what they were talking about. "Uh, sorry. What did you say?"

Quinn sighed and guided him over to a stone bench. "We need to talk."

Cade turned to look back toward the calm waters of the lake, but Eric had vanished.

"It's all right. He's gone," Quinn assured him, knowing one of the team would follow Strada.

"But where to?" Cade muttered.

"He's not my concern at the moment. You are." Quinn gently shoved him down on the bench and knelt in front of him to take his hands. "Agreeing to meet him was a stupid thing to do."

"I know." Cade found it hard to look Quinn in the eye. "He said he was going to return my gear." Cade shook his head. "No, I didn't believe him. I wanted to, but I knew he was talking out of his ass."

"So why did you agree to meet him?" Quinn looked confused.

"Because you walked away from me," Cade mumbled.

Quinn rocked back on his heels. "You agreed to meet the man who's assaulted you, to get back at me?"

Put like that, it sounded pretty dumb.

"It was a stupid thing to do," Cade said. "I didn't think."

"No, you didn't," Quinn said harshly. "You put your life in danger because you were pissed at me."

"I didn't think he'd do anything to me in public," Cade protested, hating how feeling like a little boy being scolded by his parent gave him a thrill. He'd never had anyone in his life care whether he lived or died. Even his manager only cared how much money Cade made her. Quinn sounded as if he cared. Except, he was being paid to. It wasn't real. It wasn't fucking real.

He stood, tugging his hands out of Quinn's. "It's my decision who I see. Not yours."

Quinn stood and looked down at him, and now there was only anger in his expression; the tenderness had vanished. "If you can't cooperate with me, then my job is finished. I'll contact CDR. They can replace me today."

Shock washed through Cade and he stared at Quinn. "What?"

"I can't work with clients who won't listen or agree to basic rules about their safety. Jace will escort you home. I'm done, Mr. Connolly."

Chapter Eleven

Quinn

Quinn saw the color drain from Cade's face, leaving it ashen. He tensed, ready to catch Cade if he fainted.

"You're firing me as your client?" Cade demanded.

"Yes."

"You can't do that."

Quinn crossed his arms over his chest. "I think you'll find I can. CDR contracts give me the right to walk away from non-cooperative clients."

"Quinn—"

He shook his head. "No. I take my job seriously, Mr. Connolly. And I expect my clients to do the same. You obviously can't do that. You need to find someone else. CDR will be in touch. I'll collect my things and Mogs."

It hurt Quinn to call him Mr. Connolly. He saw how Cade blossomed being called 'Boy,' but Cade flinched at the formal address.

"You can't." Cade's voice was barely above a whisper.

"Can't what?"

"Can't leave me. Can't take Mogs. You're my bodyguard."

Quinn ignored the comment about the cat. Much as he felt sorry for Cade, he wouldn't give up his Mogs to anyone.

"I've explained my reasons for leaving. I'm sure you'll find someone else who's suitable."

"You're supposed to be my Daddy."

"You left your 'Daddy' to go visit with your ex-Daddy," Quinn said. "What does that tell him about my relationship with you?"

"I didn't think of that," Cade admitted.

"You didn't think, Cade," Quinn said, weary now. Leaving Cade was going to hurt, even after such a short period of time. He needed to get away before his heart got any more involved.

Too late!

He told his traitorous heart to pipe down and looked over at Jace who stood nearby, keeping guard. He waved at him to come over. Jace looked surprised but he jogged down the path to greet them.

"Padraig is—" He stopped as Quinn interrupted.

"Jace, please escort Mr. Connolly home and arrange for one of the team to stay in the house at all times."

Jace didn't react beyond a slow blink at the 'Mr. Connolly', but Quinn knew from past experience he was going to be questioned later.

Quinn clenched his jaw. "I need to talk to Dominic. I'll be back shortly."

"Understood. Come on, Cade."

Cade reached out but Quinn ignored his hand. "Quinn, please."

"Take him home, Jace."

Quinn walked away, not bothering to see what happened. He pulled out his phone and dialed Dominic's number.

"Trouble in paradise?" Dominic's acerbic tone was like sandpaper over a road rash.

"How the hell do you know that already?" Quinn rasped.

"Jace messaged Doug, who called me," Dominic said, like it was obvious. "You need to take your boy in hand."

Quinn grunted. "We've had this conversation. He's not my boy. You need to replace me. I can't work with a client who doesn't cooperate." He stared out over the lake, oblivious to the peace and beauty around him.

"No."

"What do you mean, no?" Quinn bit out. "It's in the contract. I can walk away at any time."

"Let me phrase it differently. No."

Quinn clenched his jaw. "Let me phrase this simply. Fuck you!"

"Finished?"

Quinn did not appreciate being treated like a child having a tantrum.

"What the hell is going on, Dominic? You've never made me stay with a client if I've asked to leave."

"One, you've never quit on a job. Two, where are your balls, man? He's a scared, spoiled kid who needs taking in hand. Do it."

"He's a celebrity kid who's been badly abused. You need someone else to play the boyfriend."

"Did Strada make you?"

"I don't think so. He knows me and my rep. He thinks

I'm a loser for letting Cade—Connolly—out of my sight, but he still thinks I'm his Daddy."

"Good. Then I don't need to change anything," Dominic said with satisfaction.

"Dominic—"

"Quinn, he's connected with you. You know he has."

"He's ignoring my instructions," Quinn said. "Last night and now. I can't work like this."

"Since when did you become a diva?"

That stung. Quinn was no diva. He was a professional bodyguard.

"I don't have anyone else to take him over. Griff is busy, Craig is on assignment in Paris, and Mo isn't returning my calls."

"Then—"

"Incoming!" Jace yelled.

Quinn turned to see Cade charging toward him. He just had time to brace himself, when it didn't look like Cade was going to stop. Cade slammed into him, Quinn staggered back, and his phone went flying into the lake, Dominic calling his name.

Cade curled his fingers into Quinn's jacket and hung onto him like his life depended on it. "Don't go. Please don't go. I'll do whatever you want. I'll obey your orders. Just don't leave me." The words came out as a flying babble, barely coherent.

Quinn put his hands over Cade, who clearly thought Quinn was going to pry him away because he hung on even tighter, begging him to stay.

"Cade, calm down." When it had no noticeable effect, he barked, "Boy!"

Cade's eyes went wide, and the babbling stopped. He licked his lips. "Sorry, I—"

Quinn placed a finger over his mouth, feeling a sneaky lick. "Boy, you need to calm down. People are looking at you."

No one was close to them. To outsiders it would have looked like Quinn had to make a phone call and Cade got sick of waiting. At least, Quinn hoped that was how it looked. Cade didn't need any negative publicity before the event.

"I don't care what they see," Cade declared. "I just want you to tell me you're not leaving."

Quinn looked at his pleading eyes and took a leap off the cliff. "Daddy."

Cade's eyes went wide. "What?"

"I just want you to tell me you're not leaving, Daddy."

"You mean..."

Quinn waited.

Cade licked his lips again. "Daddy." He sounded as if he were about to pass out and his hands trembled under Quinn's.

"From now on you call me Daddy, unless we're in public with the band. Then I'm your overly possessive boyfriend. You don't leave my side. You *don't* meet Strada under any circumstances. You do exactly what I tell you or there will be consequences."

"I will," Cade promised breathlessly.

Quinn raised an eyebrow. "Boy?"

Cade bit down on his bottom lip. "I have to know before I do. Is this real or just until you catch whoever's doing this?"

"Is it a dealbreaker if I say I don't know yet?" Quinn asked.

"No." Cade looked resigned, but he said, "Don't make promises just because you think I want to hear them."

"I won't do that," Quinn agreed.

"You'll show me what it's like to have a real Daddy?"

"Yes." Quinn brought Cade's hands to his heart. "I won't treat you like Strada did."

"Then I'll take whatever you give me." Cade gave a wry smile. "You take good care of me."

"What is your safeword?" Before anything happened, he needed to know that.

"Picasso."

Quinn wasn't surprised. "Thank you for trusting me with it."

"I need to know what you expect me to do, but could we talk back home?" Cade asked, looking wiped out. "I know you'll have a list of jobs for me to do."

Quinn frowned. "Your only job is to focus on being ready for the event. You're working long hours. I don't expect you to add domestic chores on top of that. I'll organize a housekeeper for you."

"Eric expected me to clean for him."

"I know you said that before," Quinn said grimly. "Forget him. Focus on what I say."

Cade expelled a long breath and buried into Quinn's arms. "It's going to take me a while to adjust."

"I know. I'm not complicated. I don't expect you to jump through hoops. I just want you to understand that I'm not him."

Quinn nudged Cade in the direction of Jace, who was still waiting patiently by the railing. "Are you okay to ride back or do you want Jace to take your bike?"

"I'm okay. We'll take it slow."

"I trust you to know your own limits," Quinn said.

"That was something Eric never did," Cade murmured.

"What?"

"Trust me on anything."

It would have been easy to point out that Cade hadn't exactly excelled in the trust department, but he didn't want to stress Cade out even more. Quinn would show by example, and the first was trusting that Cade could get home safely.

Jace raised an eyebrow at Quinn, who gave a curt nod.

"We're going home."

"I'll follow you back." Jace said. "I'll organize a new phone for you."

Quinn had forgotten the watery fate of his phone, he'd been so focused on Cade.

He let Cade set the pace as they rode home. It was nice, basking in the late afternoon sunshine. Maybe they could spend more time on the beach once the event was over. He wouldn't be coming back to the Japanese Garden, now he knew Strada came here.

The gates of Cade's house opened as they approached and the bikes rumbled in, the higher pitch of Jace's Kawasaki behind him. Quinn and Cade headed to the garage.

Cade cut the engine and his shoulders slumped. "I don't think I could have managed much further."

"How about a nap while I make you tomato soup and grilled cheese?" Quinn suggested.

"Sounds good." Cade gave a huge yawn, then swung his leg over his bike. "Jeez, I feel like a five-year-old."

Quinn leaned forward and Cade leaned in to listen. "You don't look like a five-year-old," he murmured, pleased when Cade shivered in response.

"You're a wicked man, Daddy," Cade murmured.

"Oh yes," Quinn agreed.

In the house, Mogs screamed her displeasure at Quinn

for having to wait for her dinner, while she bequeathed Cade with purrs and wreathing around his legs.

"Tart," Quinn muttered.

Cade chuckled as he bent down to scratch her behind the ears. "She loves you best."

"Only because I feed her." Quinn had long been resigned to the role of bearer of smelly food to the Queen.

Cade yawned again. "I think I will have a nap."

"I'll feed Mogs and I'll come up and check you're all right. Doug did a sweep around the house before we arrived." He'd received that information on the route home.

Cade looked relieved. "It does make me feel better."

Quinn tugged Cade in for a quick kiss, which turned slightly more heated when Cade melted into his arms. Cade tasted of salt and wind. Finally, Quinn raised his head and looked down at Cade's glazed eyes and cherry-red lips. "You make me lose my head," he muttered.

"Good, at least it's not just me."

"It's not just you," Quinn agreed. "Go on with you."

Cade smiled shyly and ran up the stairs. Quinn watched him go.

"This has to be the worst idea ever," he muttered as he followed Mogs into the kitchen.

Cade

Was this going to be the worst idea ever?

Cade didn't know and he didn't care. He'd thrown himself at Quinn and begged him to stay so, at this point, his dignity was out the window. All he knew was, Quinn had said yes.

What if he hadn't asked? Cade wrapped his arms

around himself. Quinn could have walked away, and Cade would never have seen him again.

"You asked, and he said yes." Cade smiled. "I can call him Daddy." That would take some getting used to. In his head, Eric was still Daddy. No matter what he'd done. He needed to talk to Quinn and explain he might slip up. The one thing he was sure about was that Quinn wouldn't shout or curse or hit him if Cade needed time for something.

"Hey. You okay?" Quinn joined him in the bedroom, looking a little concerned. He'd taken time to change into a long-sleeved T-shirt and sweats. "Are you going to nap?"

Cade realized he was still standing in the bedroom, hugging himself. He straightened and tried to relax his arms. "I'm okay. Just thinking."

Quinn tugged him over to the bed and pushed him down. "Give your brain a rest and nap."

"Will you stay with me until I fall asleep?"

God, Cade sounded like a needy piece of crap. But the thought of being on his own made him feel scared.

But Quinn smiled at him like it was no big deal and nodded. "Sure. Move over, and I'll spoon around you."

Cade did as he was told, and Quinn fitted his large frame around Cade's. Quinn pressed a kiss to the nape of Cade's neck. "Sleep for a little while. I'm here."

Cade closed his eyes. Mogs jumped onto the bed and settled against him, purring quietly. For the first time for a long while, the fuzz in his brain eased. He felt safe in Quinn's arms and he could sleep knowing Quinn wouldn't leave him before he was ready.

* * *

Cade woke to the vibration of a phone. He blinked sleepily and opened his eyes to see Quinn still next to him, wearing wire-rimmed glasses, a book open on his chest and Mogs on his lap, as he reached for the phone. Quinn looked at the screen, frowned and put it back on the nightstand.

"Hey," Cade managed.

The frown slipped away from Quinn's face to be replaced by a tender smile. "Hi there."

"What's wrong?" Cade asked, rolling over onto his side to face Quinn. He didn't know how long he'd slept but it was dark outside.

"Nothing. How are you feeling now?"

Something in Quinn's voice made Cade think he was being evasive, but he decided he'd ask later when he was more awake. "Better. Have you been here the whole time?"

"No, I made dinner, then I came back up here to read in case you needed me."

Cade couldn't get over how thoughtful Quinn was. Eric would never have done the same. Maybe he was being unfair to Eric. They'd spent most of their time together going out to be seen.

"Hey." Quinn smoothed the skin between Cade's brows. "Why are you frowning? What are you thinking about?"

"Nothing important," Cade said hastily. "How long have I been asleep?"

Quinn frowned as if he didn't believe Cade but he said, "A couple of hours, that's all."

Cade reached up with one finger and touched the arm of Quinn's glasses. "I haven't seen these before."

To his amusement, Quinn looked embarrassed. "I don't have to wear them much when I'm working. I need them for reading. I guess I'm getting old."

"I wore glasses as a kid," Cade admitted, "but I got laser work done so I don't have to wear glasses or contact lenses."

"How cool."

Cade grimaced. "It was part of my manager's make-over. I got my teeth fixed too."

"Did the others get work done?"

Cade gave him a look. "Have you seen Keith?"

Quinn gave a chuckle. "I guess not. So why did you get the full treatment?"

"They needed a front man for the band. They thought I was the right candidate. They just wanted me to look pretty. I didn't mind. No one gave a crap about my teeth or eyes when I was in the system."

Quinn moved the book onto the nightstand, took off his glasses, and placed them on top of the book. He shifted Mogs between them, despite her protests, and rolled onto his side to face Cade. "You're gorgeous inside and out."

"Do you really mean that?" Cade needed to know Quinn wasn't just saying that because he thought it was what Cade wanted to hear.

"I don't play games, boy." Quinn focused all his attention on Cade. "I won't give you false flattery. I won't pander to you. If I compliment you, it's because you deserve it."

"Thank you." And Cade meant it. He liked to know where he stood with people. He'd spent his entire life moving from home to home, walking on eggshells because he didn't know how people were going to react. Straight-talkers were rare. Nowadays, most people lied to his face while stabbing him in the back.

"Let's go downstairs and eat dinner," Quinn said.

Cade wasn't really hungry, but even after two days he knew better than to say that to Quinn. The man loved with food. Cade gasped. Where the hell had that thought come from? Quinn gave him a quizzical look and Cade shook his head.

"Just a silly thought. Let's eat."

"Change into pajamas or sweats," Quinn suggested.

Cade realized he'd fallen asleep with his leathers on. "Yeah. Do I have to go out tonight?"

"No. I cleared your schedule so you can rest this evening. You've got publicity for the event tomorrow with the local radio stations, and you've got meetings with your PR guys and Louis Romero. Some guy called Joseph Holder called. I told him you'd call back." At Cade's grimace, he nodded. "Yeah, he sounded a bit of a prick. What does he want?"

"He wants to sponsor me."

"Isn't that a good thing?"

"Not if he wants to own my soul." Cade stood and stretched. "He thinks he's a Daddy. He's not, but he's convinced throwing a lot of money at me will make me cave."

He turned in time to see a flash of something cross Quinn's face that he recognized as anger. Quinn did not like the idea of someone else being interested in his boy.

"Is he hassling you?" Quinn demanded.

"He's persistent," Cade said.

He pulled out green plaid pajama bottoms and a faded, green, long-sleeved T-shirt. It was a relief to get out of the leathers. He must have been really tired not to realize he still wore them when he fell asleep.

"I'll have a word with Mr. Holder."

"It's just business," Cade said, his voice muffled as he pulled the T-shirt over his head. "I'm not interested, and he knows it."

"He needs to know you have a Daddy."

Oh yeah, from that growl, Quinn was pissed. Cade turned and smiled at him. "You'll scare the crap out of him."

Quinn walked over and cupped Cade's jaw. "I'll make my point." He rasped his thumb over the bristles on Cade's chin. "I think we both need a shave."

Cade grimaced. "I don't usually bother when I'm at home because my skin is so thin, but I'm meeting people tomorrow so I'd better make the effort."

"Do you like being shaved?"

"I've never been shaved by anyone," Cade said.

Quinn nodded. "I'll shave you. I like shaving men... all over."

Cade stared at him. "You mean—?"

"I like my men smooth."

Cade had little enough body hair that it had never occurred to him to remove the underarm hair and the small patch at the base of his cock. "Okay," he said, somewhat breathlessly.

"We'll take it slow," Quinn said. "Tonight, I'll just shave your chin. Come on, let's eat first."

As Cade followed Quinn out of the bedroom, he mused there was a worse way to spend an evening.

Chapter Twelve

Quinn

Quinn stomped down the stairs, unaccountably angry at the thought of some wannabe Daddy annoying his boy. In fact, the more he thought about it, the angrier he got. How many of these idiots had tried to entrap his boy over the years? Mr. Holder would be receiving a visit from CDR with a suggestion he ceased and desisted before Quinn ripped his head off.

"You know you're growling again, don't you?" Cade said, sounding amused.

Quinn huffed and took a deep breath to calm himself before he behaved like a complete idiot. Joseph Holder could wait. Tonight he would focus on his boy.

"Would you like to play videogames or watch TV while I finish off dinner?" At Cade's hesitation he raised an eyebrow. "Just say it."

"Would you mind if I draw?"

"Of course not."

Cade smiled gratefully. "I need to clear my mind after today."

"Cooking does it for me."

"Is it okay if I draw in the kitchen?"

"I'd like that," Quinn said, and Cade's smile grew brighter.

Cade veered off into the den while Quinn went into the kitchen. Quinn had made vegetarian chili earlier so he didn't have much to do, but he decided to stretch things out to give Cade time to relax with his drawing. He'd already fed the team. Now, he could always start on the prep for tomorrow's breakfast. The security team had made it plain that they expected more than oatmeal tomorrow. He'd pointed out he wasn't a fry cook and they'd told him to shut up and get back to the kitchen. In all honesty, if they were watching his boy's back like they had today, he would happily cook for them all.

Cade wandered into the kitchen with a large pad and a pack of pencils. He wore a puzzled look. "Have you been in the den today?"

"Yeah, I was in there earlier. Why?"

"I can't find my pens."

"I don't remember seeing them, but we could go look after dinner."

"I hope I haven't lost them. The pens have sentimental value. They were the first things I bought when I signed my first contract."

He didn't seem that worried though as he settled on a barstool. Quinn watched him out of the corner of his eye, not wanting to make him self-conscious, but Cade seemed oblivious, flipping open his pad and starting to draw with rapt concentration. Quinn moved around the kitchen with quiet efficiency, even if most of his attention was on Cade.

He wondered if Cade even realized that when he wanted to think he sucked his thumb. Probably not. It seemed such an unconscious act.

Finally, Quinn couldn't put off eating any longer. He told Cade to put away the pad and pens, which Cade did with a little huff, as Quinn served the chili into bowls and tipped the tortilla chips into another bowl.

"I usually draw while I eat," Cade complained.

"You'll have to wait until afterward," Quinn said firmly.

Cade took on a mutinous look, but Quinn had been dealing with bratty boys for a long time, so he waited, one eyebrow raised. Cade stared him out, then he dropped his gaze and pushed the pad and pens to one side.

"Good boy."

He served the meal, making sure the sour cream, cheese, and guacamole were in reach.

"This looks good," Cade said, diving into the food with undisguised enthusiasm.

Quinn loved cooking for someone who enjoyed their food as much as he did. Most of his boys hadn't been interested in his talents in the kitchen. Cooking for Cade and the team was a real pleasure. Maybe not the team so much.

As Cade scarfed the chili, Quinn said, "How are you feeling now?"

"Since I discovered Eric and Batty Brenda aren't my only stalkers?" Put like that, Cade sounded remarkably calm.

"Yes."

"I don't know. I'm used to the uber-fans, and they're more annoying than scary. Some of them are quite sweet. Brenda's just persistent. As for Eric, I'm starting to feel sorry for him. I think he's realized he can't just snap his fingers and I'll crawl back to him. Is there more chili?"

Quinn wanted to melt. His boy had the sweetest of hearts under the spiky exterior but how could he be so blind to the danger Strada presented?

"Quinn?"

Quinn blinked. "Sorry?"

"Is there more chili?" Cade asked. "Are you okay? You're not eating."

"I'm fine. Sorry, I was lost in thought. Give me your bowl."

"I can serve myself," Cade protested.

"I always serve my boys," Quinn pointed out as he filled the empty bowl. He heard Cade's breath hitch.

"Your boys?"

"You're my boy, aren't you?"

Silence hung between them for a moment, then Cade said shakily, "I know I keep asking but I need the reassurance. I am *your* boy, yes? I mean for now. You won't be taking any other boys?"

Quinn sat down and took one of Cade's hands. He squeezed it gently before letting go. "It'll be just you."

Cade stared down at the bowl of food steaming in front of him. "Don't break my heart, Quinn. I don't think I could take that again."

What did Quinn say to that? He hadn't said he was in love with Cade. Cade hadn't said he was in love with Quinn.

"I don't know why I said that," Cade muttered. "My brain is all turned around after today."

Quinn nodded and started eating his dinner. They ate in uncomfortable silence and Quinn had to find some way to resolve the situation. "I can't promise not to break your heart, my boy. But I promise not to hurt you like Strada did. If it helps to know, I stay friends with my former boys."

"As long as they are just friends." And even if the smile didn't quite reach his eyes, Cade made the effort to be a brat. "When are you gonna shave me?"

"Let's do that after I clear up," Quinn suggested, pleased to have something else to focus on.

"I can help you."

Cade took his plate to the sink, rinsed it off, and placed it in the dishwasher. Quinn cleared the counter and they worked together for a few minutes until the remainder of the chili was covered and waiting to cool down before it went in the fridge, and the dishwasher hummed as it worked.

"I like helping," Cade said. "We all had to help in the foster homes. I've gotten used to it."

"I prefer creating the mess to clearing it up," Quinn admitted, "but I've been on my own for a long time and Mogs isn't going to clear up for me." He caught Cade's grin and they both chuckled.

"You could buy her a little apron," Cade suggested.

"*You* buy her the apron and good luck getting it on her." Quinn pushed up one of his sleeves and showed Cade his arm. The pink stripes were clear through the inked skin. "These are from trying to give her pills."

Cade offered his arm. He had nearly a matching set. "Charlie was the same."

"Damn cats." Quinn grinned at him. "Come on then. Time to be a smooth boy."

And yes, he took great satisfaction in the full body shudder from Cade.

Cade

Cade chewed the inside of his lip as he watched Quinn's preparations. His eyes opened wide when he saw the straight razor in Quinn's bag.

"I don't think I need that," he said, pointing at the razor.

"It's a sensual experience being shaved with a razor as sharp as this," Quinn said.

"No way. That razor is going nowhere near my throat."

The disappointed look Quinn gave him made him want to fall on his knees and beg Quinn's forgiveness.

"I'll let it go this time," Quinn said, "but I hope in time you'll trust me enough to use this razor on you."

Cade thought about it as Quinn pulled a pack of safety razors out. Quinn could have shouted and insisted shaving Cade with the straight razor, but he didn't. Quinn's gentleness when he expected aggression messed with Cade's head. Why was an alpha man like Quinn so gentle with him?

"Sit down here," Quinn said, pointing to the edge of the bath.

Cade sat down gingerly and waited. He'd never been shaved before. He preferred a light stubble, which he maintained himself when he was performing, feeling it gave him a rakish look, rather than the boyish one when he was clean-shaven. He was always carded when he shaved and, at twenty-three, he'd had enough of that. He'd mentioned that to Quinn, who had hummed and assured him that there wouldn't be a hair on his chin when he'd finished. So, ignored him then. Cade wasn't sure how he felt about this, but the thought of Quinn's hands on him made his dick harden. Quinn pressed a hot washcloth to his face. Cade closed his eyes, feeling the heat seep through him.

"I'm just doing your face today," Quinn said. "We'll work through your body."

Cade still wasn't sure he liked the idea of a razor going anywhere near his cock. "I still don't see why I need to lose my hair. It's not like I'm furry."

"Because it's sensual, and you're going to lose your mind when I lick you all over."

Quinn took the washcloth away and started lathering Cade's face with shaving gel. He looked into Cade's eyes. "Just relax. I'll never hurt you."

"I know that," Cade said.

And he did, even after all the hurt he'd had in his life.

The rasp of the razor was shockingly loud in the small room, but Quinn's hands were gentle as he slowly stroked the razor over Cade's jaw.

"You're so beautiful," Quinn murmured, his voice soothing Cade's jangled nerves.

Cade hummed but stayed still. Because, razor!

Then Quinn took the washcloth again and wet it to wipe Cade's face clean. "You can look in the mirror."

Cade stared at his reflection. He looked so young without the stubble. "I look about twelve."

Quinn chuckled as he cleared everything away. "Oh no. I'm not interested in kids. You're all man, baby."

Cade preened under his praise. He got to his feet and stretched. "We could watch a movie in bed."

"I'd like that," Quinn agreed.

They stripped down to briefs and curled up on the bed, Cade not hesitating when Quinn offered him a cuddle. Mogs settled down next to them, purring happily when Quinn petted her. Cade wished he could purr like her.

"What do you want to watch?" Cade asked.

"I'm not really into movies," Quinn confessed. "I prefer reading."

"Old-timer," Cade teased.

Quinn wrinkled his nose. "Just old."

"You're not old, Daddy!" Cade nipped at Quinn's chin, then held his breath, taken aback at his own bravery.

"I feel it sometimes," Quinn admitted, "but thank you, my boy."

"You're perfect."

Cade sighed and leaned against Quinn. He felt a kiss brush the top of his head and tilted his head so he could have a proper kiss. Quinn groaned low in his throat and then Cade found himself on top of Quinn and looking down. Quinn cupped Cade's neck and tugged him down. Unlike the other times this wasn't Quinn playing to an audience. He genuinely wanted to kiss Cade. The kiss was deep and wet and dirty, and Cade never wanted it to stop.

"I've wanted to do this for so long," Cade confessed when they eventually pulled back.

Quinn smiled at him. "You've kissed me before."

"But not like this. Not for real. You kissed me to prove a point to Eric."

"Kissing you has never been an act. I've wanted to kiss you since the first moment I met you."

Cade stared down at his huge brown eyes. There was no deceit there. "I could fall for you so easy," he whispered.

Too late, his mind whispered back.

"What do you want to do?" Quinn asked.

In that moment, Cade knew he could say he wanted to go to sleep, or ask Quinn to sleep in the other room, and Quinn would do it.

"I want to suck your cock, Daddy."

Quinn nodded. "I'd love your mouth around my cock, boy."

Cade wriggled down until he was facing Quinn's cotton covered bulge. From the way the tip of his cock was poking over the waistband, Quinn's dick was just as happy with the idea. As he watched, a pear-shaped drop of liquid formed in the slit. He bent to taste it, groaning at the salty-sweet flavor. He mouthed along the thick shaft still covered by the cotton. It was good but not enough. He tugged on the briefs and pulled them down, settling between Quinn's thighs. Quinn's cock was flushed purple and his heavy sac made Cade's mouth water.

"You don't have to do this if you don't want to," Quinn assured him.

Cade looked up. Quinn looked concerned.

"I really want to," he said.

"If you're sure."

Suddenly Cade didn't want to be handled with kid gloves anymore.

"Order me to suck your cock, please, Daddy," he begged.

Quinn's eyes darkened. "Suck my cock, boy!"

Heat unfurled through Cade at his growl. He wanted this. He needed it so much. He took as much of Quinn's cock into his mouth as he could manage, loving Quinn's groan above him.

Quinn's fingers tangled in his hair, the tug adding an edge of pain that heightened his senses. "You're so good at this."

Cade knew how to suck cock, knew how to make a man feel good, and he employed each one of the skills he knew to drive Quinn to the point of distraction. Quinn clearly loved having his dick sucked, from the way he moaned when

Cade dipped into the slit and swirled his tongue around the glans. All the time, he praised Cade for making him feel good. Cade cupped Quinn's sac and sucked on the head, going as far down as he could go.

"I need to come, boy," Quinn ordered.

Cade sucked harder, sinking down, his throat muscles closing around the tip of Quinn's cock. He gagged and pulled back. The one practical part of his brain reminded him he couldn't wreck his voice for the event, but he did everything he could with his mouth and hands to make Quinn forget his name.

"Cade. Boy. God."

Cade looked up to see Quinn staring at him with fierce pleasure. He sank back down, making sure he never took his eyes off his Daddy. Then Quinn's eyes rolled back, and he arched his back, coming in Cade's mouth. Cade swallowed fast, taking Quinn's come with pleasure. He stayed there until Quinn had quieted, not moving until Quinn tugged him up to kiss him hard and lick around the inside of his mouth.

Someone likes the taste of himself.

He would remember that for the future. Maybe save a mouthful to share with Quinn.

Then Quinn shoved Cade onto his back and, before Cade knew what was happening, his briefs were tugged down and Quinn gave him the fastest blowjob he'd ever received. It was over embarrassingly quickly, Quinn's hands pushing him down into the bed as he spurted over Quinn's face. That was so hot, especially when Quinn licked his lips. Cade grabbed Quinn's chin to clean him off with gentle licks. They were both messy with come and sweat.

Quinn collapsed back on the pillows and stared up at the ceiling. "I think I just ran a marathon."

Cade giggled and curled up against him. They both needed a shower, but it could wait. Sated and happy, Cade was on the edge of sleep when he felt Quinn, who was wrapped around him, stiffen.

"What's wrong?" Cade asked sleepily.

"I heard a noise."

Cade hadn't heard a thing. "The house creaks sometimes."

"I'm just going to do a check and I'll be back," Quinn promised with a quick kiss to Cade's cheek, then he slid out of bed.

"Don't be long," Cade said.

"I won't."

Cade thought about joining him, but he'd be in the way. He listened as Quinn padded down the stairs. His Daddy took such good care of him.

Please let me be able to keep him.

Chapter Thirteen

Quinn

Quinn had tentative plans for the following day after Cade's meetings, but Cade seemed distracted and out of sorts. After breakfast, Cade said he was canceling all the meetings and spending the day in the studio. Oh well, Quinn's plans could wait. He cleared away the breakfast dishes. In the middle of loading the dishwasher, he heard footsteps behind him. To his disappointment, Gareth stood in the doorway.

Quinn raised an eyebrow. "Is everything okay?"

"Just checking to see if you need me today. The record company need an extra driver."

"Go for it. I don't know if Cade wants to go out, but we can get a car."

Hopefully we'll be using two wheels, not four.

Gareth smiled and disappeared, only to be replaced by Cade who gave him a shy smile. "I wondered if you'd come sit with me in the studio. I feel a bit lonely."

"Do you have to rehearse now?" Quinn asked.

"No. I'm ready for the gig. I just have some thinking to do and playing my guitar helps."

"Want a change of scene?"

Cade raised an eyebrow. "Like what?"

"Let's take the bikes out."

Quinn saw the excitement in Cade's eyes.

"Both bikes?"

"Why not?"

"I thought I was on house arrest."

Quinn snorted. That theory would have been great if Cade had complied. "I've got us some backup."

Cade's eyes narrowed. "Like the CDR team?"

"Among others," Quinn agreed.

Jace and Padraig would be there, but so would his brothers.

Cade looked unsure and Quinn grinned at him.

"We both need to get out of here."

"Where are you thinking?"

"It's a surprise. Full leathers. We're going to be on the Hogs all day."

His boy gave a positive shimmy of excitement. "I can't wait."

"Get ready. We've got to leave soon."

Cade bolted out of the kitchen and up the stairs. Quinn listened to make sure he was out of earshot before he called Doug.

"It's a go."

"Are you sure about this?" Doug asked.

"Yes. We need to be seen together, and Strada's got the message now."

"You hope."

"If he hasn't, I'll make sure he gets it."

"You're a thug," Doug said.

"Yeah." Quinn knew exactly what he was. He also didn't care.

"Jace and Padraig are ready." Doug snorted. "They're like little kids at being given the Harleys."

"Did you tell them they have to give them back?"

"Yeah. They gave me a message to give to you."

Quinn grinned. "Oh?"

"You've got to catch them first."

"We'll be out in fifteen minutes," Quinn said, and disconnected the call before he chuckled. He'd have given anything to see the two operatives' faces when they saw the bikes. They may talk the talk about their racing bikes, but give them a Hog and they were like kids in a candy store.

He met Cade in the entry ten minutes later. They were both in black leathers, helmets under their arms.

"Where are we going?" Cade asked.

"Wait and see." Quinn opened the door and Cade gasped at Jace and Padraig on the Harleys in front of the steps.

"What the hell?"

"We're gonna meet up with my chapter. These two had to be riding Harleys."

Cade chewed on his bottom lip. "I don't know. I thought we were going by ourselves."

Was that disappointment in his voice?

Quinn laid his arm over Cade's shoulders. "You're safe, boy. The chapter is all LGBT+ friendly."

It would do Cade good to meet with other people where he didn't have to pretend, and his chapter welcomed anyone in the community.

Cade blinked. "All gay men?"

"Women too. We travel a long way for a once a month

meet. I wasn't going to go this month, but we're as safe as we can be, surrounded by my brothers and sisters."

"I never rode with anyone else. Eric didn't like me riding my bike with anyone except him, and the management team always made a fuss."

Quinn curled his lip. "I figured as much. Which is good because Strada's unlikely to interfere, and you get to do something you love." He hugged Cade against him. "Still want to go?"

Cade tilted his head to look at him. "I never met a bodyguard who let me have so much fun."

Quinn ached for him. Cade was still so young, and in the spotlight all the time. He needed time to enjoy life too.

* * *

Quinn watched his boy unfurl like a butterfly in the sunshine. Cade had been reserved and quiet when Quinn had introduced him to the chapter, but once he discovered they really didn't care he was a celebrity, and the only thing they cared about was the Harley, he relaxed, and it didn't take long before he was in a heated discussion with half a dozen others about... Quinn didn't have a clue what they were talking about, he was just happy that Cade was enjoying himself.

Jace and Padraig stayed close by, not getting involved. Quinn played the possessive asshole boyfriend. Despite what Quinn had said, he didn't trust Strada not to take another pop at Cade. As far as the whole world was concerned, Cade was his, and it was obvious Cade loved it, loved being owned by him. Could Quinn give him up when this was over?

"Quinn?"

He started at Cade mentioning his name. "Huh, what did I miss?"

Cade chuckled. "Mo asked if you were ready to move out?"

"You're getting old," Mo mocked.

"You're older than me, dickwad." Quinn received a mocking laugh. Mo was the closest thing to a big brother he had, and treated him like it. Mo was also a Daddy, but he'd lost his boy three years before to an accident and he swore that part of his life was over. Quinn was just grateful Mo still attended the chapter.

It was interesting. Cade hadn't reacted to Mo's obvious dominance in the same way he had to Quinn's, back at CDR. Was that because Quinn had focused his attention on Cade, making Cade feel safe?

"Where are we going?" Cade asked.

Quinn hugged him close. "Wherever Mo takes us."

Mo grinned. "Glad to see you know your place."

Cade shook his head as he glanced between the two of them. "Are you always like this?"

"Usually they're worse." A butch lesbian joined them, her face already pinking from the sun and wind. "They're on their best behavior because you're here."

Quinn and Mo both scoffed but maybe Joanie had a point. They were usually bitching at each other the whole journey, just because they could.

Once they were on the road, Quinn felt any tension drain away. Being here with his family was essential for his mental health, just as it was for them. He looked at Cade who grinned the most genuine smile he'd ever seen. Quinn chalked it up as a win. One more thing he'd done right for his boy.

By the time they reached the roadside bar, Quinn felt

his nose itching from the sun, and his mind relaxed from the ride. It was a perfect day. Cade rumbled up beside him, Jace and Padraig flanking them. Even the two gruff bodyguards looked happy.

The chapter came to the bar every month. The owner had no issue with them being LGBT or bikers. He just insisted on no trouble. One strike and you were out. The chapter abided by that, as most of them had jobs where they couldn't afford bad publicity.

Quinn took off his helmet and shook out his hair. Cade did the same, pushing back the sweaty strands.

"Burgers and wings? Tacos for me and Cade?" Quinn asked, looking at Cade and the team.

"You buying?" Padraig asked.

"I thought I'd send the check to Dominic."

Padraig and Jace burst into howling laughter.

Cade looked between them. "I'm missing something."

"Dominic is notoriously tight. Yeah, I'm paying." When Cade opened his mouth, Quinn shook his head. "The day is my treat."

"If you're sure."

"I'm sure."

Jace beamed at him. "Beers on you then, Ryder."

"You're working," Quinn barked. "You got to ride the bikes. Get over it."

Padraig and Jace groaned, but Jace gave a wink to Cade as they followed the rest of the chapter into the bar.

Quinn cursed himself afterward for not being more on the ball. He'd let Cade get ahead of him which meant there was no one between Cade and everyone else.

The screech echoed around the bar. "Cade Connolly. It's Cade Connolly. O.M.G!"

Cade

One minute he'd been relishing the thought of a cold beer, and the next he was being yanked into Quinn's arms as a woman rushed toward him, waving her arms.

"Cade, Cade, it's me, Tessie. I love you, Cade."

She reached for him as Quinn spun him around and forcibly shoved him into Jace's arms, and Padraig rushed past to intercept her.

"Stay with Jace," Quinn hissed.

Jace steadied him until Cade regained his balance. "Okay?"

Cade blinked. "Yeah. What just happened there? Oh my God, is that Batty Brenda?"

"Batty Brenda?"

Cade flushed. "She's a regular. Sends me flowers."

"Aren't you the lucky boy," Jace drawled.

"Fuck you," Cade said, but without any heat.

"My girlfriend might be happy, but I'm strictly a one-woman guy."

Cade flipped him off. They were having this stupid conversation and all he wanted was a beer, while inside he could hear Tessie protesting that she knew him and only wanted to say hello.

"You need to stay away from Mr. Connolly," Quinn growled.

His Daddy was not happy.

"I thought CDR told her to stay away from me," Cade said to Jace.

Jace nodded. "They did, but I don't expect she thought for one moment she'd ever meet you."

"She has met me. At some fan event for the band. She seems to think we formed a deeper relationship then."

"From what I hear, it's not the first time."

"It comes with the territory," Cade said wryly, suddenly wiped out. Any enjoyment of the day had been sucked away. "Do you think we could go home?

"Wait a minute."

Jace waved and Padraig came out.

"What?"

"Cade wants to go home."

Padraig cocked his head as he looked at Cade. "Do you want to go home, or would you like a cool beer, wings, and no Tessie?"

"If you make it tacos, that does sound good," Cade admitted.

"How about you go in there, flatter her for two minutes, then the chapter is gonna intervene, and you get the rest of the day in your man's arms."

"You want me to talk to her?"

"Yeah. It's that or a restraining order. Let's try Mister Nice Guy first."

Cade nodded. It was good advice. He didn't like to upset fans. He took a deep breath and walked into the bar, wearing the biggest, fakest smile he could muster.

* * *

In just his T-shirt and briefs, Cade collapsed onto their bed, face down, his head buried in the covers, thankful he was not moving.

Quinn ran a hand down his back. "Are you okay, boy?"

"I'm exhausted," he admitted. "I haven't ridden like that for years."

"It was a long day."

Cade forced himself to roll over onto his back to ease the

concern he heard in Quinn's voice. "It was a great day," he declared, pleased at the smile on Quinn's face. "And yeah, even Tessie was nice once she got over the "OMG Cade Connolly!" shrieking."

"That was a nice thing you did, considering she stalked you."

"I hope we've stopped that now. And at least we know where the black roses came from."

Quinn furrowed his brow. "Why would she think you'd like black roses?"

"I think I made up some bullshit about being a goth at a recent interview." He grimaced. "I've got to quit doing that. It always comes back to bite me on the ass."

"But she denies the note."

Cade was too tired to care. All he wanted was a quiet night in. "Who knows? Maybe the note was for someone else. Do you think we could get takeout tonight?"

"You don't want me to cook?" Quinn didn't seem offended, just curious.

"I want to spend the evening in your arms," Cade admitted.

"We can do that. I'm tired too," Quinn said. "How about we nap, then order food?"

Cade moaned in appreciation. "That sounds so good."

Quinn stripped down to his briefs and settled on the bed, spooning around Cade. He brushed a kiss to the nape of Cade's neck and a moment later he was asleep, soft snores interspersed with the occasional snort.

Cade lay awake for a while, not relaxed enough to sleep. They'd solved the issue of the flowers but not the note with it. It was like every time they solved one piece of the puzzle, another presented itself.

The house creaked and he smiled at the familiar sound.

It was warm and comforting to be back in his own place, safe and warm with Quinn and Mogs. The note could wait. He needed a nap.

* * *

"Dinner! Hurry up!" Quinn bellowed at him.

"I'm coming!" Cade yelled back, irritated and not bothering to hide it.

How did nap and order food turn into Quinn cooking again? Cade had woken up to find himself alone and Quinn downstairs clattering around in the kitchen. He was going to have to talk to Quinn about this. He rubbed his hair to dry it off, taking his time because this was his house and why shouldn't he? Maybe he took a bit longer than he should, though, because he heard Quinn stomping up the stairs.

Quinn appeared in the bedroom doorway, a scowl on his face. "Didn't you hear me?"

"I heard," Cade muttered.

"What's your problem? Aren't you hungry?"

Was Quinn really that oblivious? "I asked you for takeout and a night in your arms. I wake up. You're not here. You're downstairs cooking."

Quinn blinked at the tirade. Cade felt a little guilty but not that much.

"I wasn't cooking," Quinn said calmly.

Cade hated it when Quinn used that tone on him. "I heard you."

"No, you heard Tormac cooking because I told him I wasn't cooking tonight. I've been up for fifteen minutes. Long enough to order food and bellow at Tormac."

"But you yelled 'dinner' at me."

"Just to get you moving."

Cade started to feel stupid. "You've ordered takeout?"

"I did. Thai."

Cade sighed. "I'm sorry."

"I'm sorry too." Quinn made no effort to come closer. "Why did you think you couldn't trust me?"

"You weren't here when I woke up."

"Is that all?"

"I had a nightmare," Cade admitted.

Eric had been forcing himself on Cade, who couldn't move. The dream seemed to go on and on for hours, and he'd been begging for his Daddy to wake him up, but Quinn just left him to Eric's mercies. He'd woken up with tears on his cheeks, wanting to scream, and sucking his thumb to calm down. Quinn not being there had been the last straw.

Cade spilled out the dream and before he'd gotten to the end, he was in Quinn's arms, wrapped up so tight he could barely breathe, but he was safe again.

"I'm so sorry," Quinn murmured over and over. "I'm here. You're safe. I'll never let anyone hurt you."

Cade couldn't help the few tears that squeezed between his lashes, more from relief than anything else.

They stayed locked together until the doorbell interrupted them. Quinn jumped like always, and Cade giggled.

"Stay here," Quinn ordered.

Cade nodded, wrapping his arms around himself as Quinn strode out.

"Tormac, can you get the door? Cade and I'll be down in a minute."

"Sure, what the hell was that noise?"

Cade heard Quinn mutter, "See, it's not just me." He grinned. He loved that abomination of a doorbell.

Quinn came back in, shut the door, and took Cade into his arms.

"I'm all right," Cade assured him.

"I'm sure you are but I'm a show, not tell, kind of guy." Quinn looked down at Cade. "I'm going to put you on the bed and show you that Eric doesn't have you anymore, boy. It's you and me."

"The dinner?"

"It can wait. You're more important."

Quinn undid the towel Cade had around his waist, dropping it unheeded to the floor. Then he led Cade to the bed and laid him down so gently Cade had to blink back the tears. Quinn undressed as Cade watched. His Daddy was huge and muscled and would keep him safe forever.

It wasn't how Cade expected their first time. In his imagination, Quinn had thrown him up against the wall and rammed that thick cock into him. He wanted that, one day. This time Quinn whispered in Cade's ear about how special he was as he prepared him, thick fingers driving him to distraction. Cade didn't know whether to focus on his words or his fingers. Both. Neither. He begged for Quinn to stick his cock in him, and Quinn did, slowly again, and Cade focused on that, because his Daddy was never going to hurt him like Eric had. His climax was like plunging into a clear spring pool. It took his breath away, but it cleared the last remnants of the nightmare. Quinn waited until Cade had come then he buried himself deep inside Cade and shuddered his way through his own orgasm, Cade whispering how much he loved him in his ear, because Quinn wouldn't be able to focus on it then.

Chapter Fourteen

Quinn

Quinn woke to humming and purring. He cracked open one eye to the lovely vision of the long line of Cade's back and his neat ass. Cade sat nude on the bed, his tongue peeping out the corner of his mouth while he sketched Mogs, who was stretched across the bottom of the bed. It was daylight outside, and sunlight striped the bed, bathing Mogs's fur as she basked.

Quinn couldn't resist the temptation to sweep his hand down Cade's spine and cup one ass-cheek. "Morning, boy, are you making a liar out of me?"

Cade looked over his shoulder and grinned. "Hey, you're awake. What do you mean?"

"I usually sleep lightly. Yet here you are drawing, and I slept through it."

"I bought new pens to leave in my nightstand. I want to draw."

Cade seemed to hold his breath as if he expected Quinn

to tell him it wasn't permitted, but Quinn said, "That's cool. How long have you been awake?"

"Ages. I thought you were never going to wake up."

"Yesterday wore me out," Quinn admitted. He sat up and rasped his bristles over the soft skin on Cade's shoulder.

"Hey!" Cade protested, but he shivered a little so Quinn did it again.

"You're mean, especially as I can't do that to you."

Quinn chuckled. "Not mean, just devious."

Cade turned so they could kiss, which started chaste but quickly got a little bit out of control.

"How are you this morning?" Quinn asked, when breathing became a necessity.

"My ass aches," Cade grumbled with a slight blush Quinn found adorable.

"Good," Quinn said, not remotely apologetic. He'd used his boy hard the previous night, and Cade had loved it. They'd made love three times, until their cocks sent up white flags of protest. "What are you planning to do today?"

"I've got to talk to my manager about the UK tour." Cade grimaced. "We booked it to get away from Eric, and now there's no need to go."

Quinn had been thinking about that, too. He knew Cade had to go. It would cost too much to cancel now, but the thought of being away from his boy made him feel sick. He always needed to be by Cade's side. "Maybe a change of scene would be good, though. You've had a rough time." At Cade's speculative look, he said, "What are you planning?"

"You could come with. I love London, and we could take time to explore."

"I could. I've got time owing to me. Would you like that?" He would have to find someone to take care of Mogs, of course. One minute Cade beamed at him and the next

Quinn was flattened by a very happy boy. "I take it that's a yes, then?"

"You talk to CDR, and I'll talk to my manager." Cade's expression turned predatory and Quinn waited to see what would happen next.

Mogs jumped off the bed with a huff but neither man paid attention to her. From the hot, wet kisses being peppered over his chest, Quinn deduced Cade wanted playtime. Then the kissing became more languorous, Cade's tongue sweeping around his nipple. Quinn's cock thickened at each skillful stroke of Cade's tongue. Quinn loved the fact Cade trusted him enough to take what he wanted. And he was so good at this. His boy was going to make him come before he'd even touched Quinn's cock. Quinn sighed and stretched, Cade still working his mouth over him. He settled a hand on Cade's head and lay back for the ride.

"Hey!" Quinn yelped as Cade tugged hard on one of his chest hairs. He looked down indignantly to see Cade smirking at him. "What was that for?"

"Just checking to see you were awake. Your eyes were closed."

Quinn growled, and moved suddenly, throwing his boy over his lap.

Taken off guard, Cade flailed for a moment before he subsided. He turned to glower at Quinn. "What was that for?"

"Naughty boys get their bottoms spanked."

Quinn held his breath, waiting to hear Cade's safe word. Or would Cade trust him enough to let him do this?

Cade sighed and relaxed over Quinn's lap. Most of him was relaxed. His dick was very unrelaxed, trapped between his belly and Quinn's thighs.

"Do it," Cade murmured.

Quinn waited.

"Sorry, Daddy."

"Five smacks for cheeking your Daddy. I want to hear you."

One day Quinn would spank Cade until he came, because they both wanted that. But today was a quick discipline for a cheeky brat. He laid his hand over Cade's cheek, admiring the tautness, then he laid five slaps in quick succession, leaving his hand there on the last one to soak up the warmth. Cade had given a satisfying yelp for each one, but his dick had remained hard, leaking steadily.

The silence in the room was broken only by the sound of them breathing. Then Cade said, "Please, Daddy, fuck me."

God! Yes!

But he had to check. "You said your ass was sore."

"Just don't fuck me dry, and I'll be fine," Cade said impatiently. "Come on, come on." He reached over to the nightstand to grab the rubbers and slick.

"Ride me," Quinn ordered.

"Yes, yes."

Cade fumbled with the packets. It took both of them to get the condom on; their hands were shaking. But the minute Quinn slid a finger inside Cade's ass, Cade went slack, his mouth open. It didn't take long to prepare him. Then Cade sank down to the hilt on Quinn's cock in one motion. He couldn't hide his flinch, although Quinn didn't know if it was from his channel or his reddened ass.

"Gentle, baby," Quinn said, frowning at him.

"Fuck gentle," Cade snarled at him. He was wild, his hair a tousled mess, his eyes huge, the blue barely visible.

Quinn needed to take control before he lost it for good. He flipped them up and over, burying Cade under his body.

He looked down into Cade's eyes. "I decide what you need."

He waited. Anger and frustration crossed Cade's face, then he nodded, just once. Submission obtained, Quinn fucked Cade slowly until Cade was dripping in sweat, yelling at him, and pleading for more, to stop, to go on, to never ever stop. His fingers dug into Quinn's shoulders. There would be bruises there, and Quinn relished that idea. When Quinn finally let him climax, Cade shattered into a thousand pieces, and Quinn was there to put him together.

Cade

They'd get downstairs eventually. Quinn seemed more interested in kissing him and touching him than going downstairs to make breakfast. And Cade was out of it. Truly and utterly out of it. What the hell had Quinn done to him?

They showered together and Quinn brought him to another toe-curling orgasm with his hand, then Cade dropped to his knees for a reciprocal blowjob. He was addicted to the weight and taste of his Daddy's cock in his mouth.

As they got dressed, the house creaked again. Cade ignored it, but Quinn frowned and looked up.

"I keep hearing the same noise. What do you keep in the attic?"

"I don't know, to be honest," Cade admitted. "I don't think I've been up there in years. Do you think it's an animal?" He hated the idea of an animal being trapped in the attic and he hadn't checked.

"Let's go look," Quinn said.

"Okay." Cade jumped off the bed and followed Quinn

up the attic stairs, taking the time to admire Quinn's tight butt. His Daddy was gorgeous.

He'd ignored the attic since he moved in, so it wouldn't be that surprising if a small creature had gotten in. Cade hoped it wasn't rats. He really didn't like rats. He'd almost reached the top step when Quinn suddenly stopped, his arms out, barring Cade from going any further.

"Quinn?"

"Just wait here," Quinn said in a low voice.

He went on ahead, leaving Cade waiting. Tension ratcheted in Cade at the silence from Quinn. He could hear footsteps and things moving, but Quinn didn't say anything. Cade was on the verge of disobeying Quinn when Quinn said, "Come here."

Cade walked into the attic, a long room stretching the length of the house. Quinn stood in the middle, his arms crossed, a deep frown on his face as he looked down. That was probably where his bedroom was, Cade judged.

"Quinn, what's wrong?"

"You've definitely got a visitor and one that creates holes."

"What do you think it is? Oh. What are these doing here?" Cade held up a small pack of pens to show Quinn. "These are the pens I said were missing from the den."

Quinn's face changed immediately. "Cade, go downstairs and wait in the kitchen," he ordered. "I'm going to call the team in."

Cade knew this was one of those times not to argue or play heroic. He got to his feet, still holding the pens. "Should I take them or leave them?"

"Leave them for now," Quinn said. His expression softened. "I promise you'll get them back."

Cade nodded but, despite their sentimental value, he swore he would never touch them again.

He went down the stairs and then down the main stairs to the kitchen. He could hear Quinn muttering as he waited for one of the team to answer.

He'd make coffee for everyone. It would give him something to do. Cade stopped at the sight of his driver in the kitchen.

"Hey, Gareth. What are you doing here?"

Gareth didn't usually venture into the house. Eric had made it clear he didn't want anyone else in the house—to see him hurt Cade—and Quinn had forbidden anyone coming in unless he knew about it. Unlike Eric, Quinn had gone over to the garage to have that discussion with Gareth in person, because he was a decent guy.

Cade wandered over to the coffee maker. "I'm not going anywhere today. You can have the day off if you want."

Gareth smiled at him but he didn't say anything.

Cade furrowed his brow. "Gareth, are you okay?"

"Where is he?" Gareth asked, in his soft Welsh burr.

"Quinn?"

Gareth nodded.

"He's in the attic."

Gareth smiled again, and Cade tried to return it but there was something off that made his blood run cold. He thought about calling for Quinn but he wasn't sure how Gareth would react.

"It's a shame you had to find it," Gareth said conversationally.

"Find what?" Now Cade was confused.

Gareth rolled his eyes. "I know you're a dumb pop star, but bloody hell, Cade, you ought to get it by now."

"Get what?" Cade had no idea what he was supposed to

get. What was wrong with Gareth?

"The fact that he's been living upstairs in the attic," Quinn said from the doorway, his tone like ice.

Thank God! Quinn's here. Wait! What?

Cade wanted to run over to Quinn, but he forced himself to stay where he was and focus on Gareth. "Is this true? You've lived in my attic? But you live in the garage." What was he missing?

"He's been spying on you. There are peepholes into the bathroom and the bedroom," Quinn said.

Cade's blood ran cold. "You're joking."

"No, he's right," Gareth said, and he sounded almost regretful. Almost.

"What have you done with my team?" Quinn demanded.

"You've been watching me! Why?" Cade shrieked, realizing he'd been betrayed by yet another person he thought he could trust.

"They're locked in the garage. They'll be fine. Isn't it obvious? I love you, Cade." Gareth said. "And you love me too, don't you? That's why you employed me."

Cade was stunned. Gareth had seen him with Quinn. Seen him with Eric.

"You love me?"

"Yes," Gareth said almost dreamily.

"You saw me with Eric?"

"Yes."

"You saw Eric rape me?" Cade spat.

The harsh words seem to penetrate the fugue Gareth was in. "I...no..."

"You saw him hit me? You watched!" Cade's voice went up and Quinn made a move toward him.

Gareth cut in front of Quinn. "No!"

"Get out of my way," Quinn rasped.

"Cade is mine, not yours," Gareth snarled at Quinn.

Cade realized that Gareth had snapped. Whatever was going on in his head, he'd lost the plot. "I'm flattered, Gareth, but I'm not the right kind of guy for you."

"You need a Daddy. I can be your Daddy. You just need slapping into line. He just did that, didn't he?" Gareth pointed at Quinn.

Cade stiffened. *He* watched Quinn spanking him.

Quinn shook his head. "That's the mistake a lot of men make. They think being dominant means speaking with your fists. Or worse. Whereas true dominance is understanding the gift your boy has given you. I smacked Cade because we both wanted it. But Eric abused him."

Gareth scowled at Quinn. "What gift?"

Quinn ignored Gareth as if he wasn't worth his time, and smiled at Cade. "Your submission is a gift to be cherished and nurtured."

"I never knew it could be like this," Cade murmured. "You've given me so much."

He stared into Quinn's eyes, lost in the love he saw there. Why hadn't he met Quinn first, before the innocence was beaten out of him?

"Christ, no wonder he keeps running back to Eric," Gareth sneered.

"I'm not. I don't," Cade insisted, looking at Quinn, begging him not to believe Gareth.

"Was it you who told Eric we were at the club?" Quinn asked Gareth.

Gareth grinned at Cade's gasp. "Eric was weak too. He believed me when I told him you still wanted him. Why do you think he always knew where you were?"

"Jesus." Cade stared at him. "It's been you this whole

time? You've been manipulating Eric too?"

"He's a narcissist. He'll believe anything if it makes him the center of the world."

"And you? What did you want, Long?" Quinn demanded.

"Control," Gareth said, not taking his eyes off Cade. "I'm going to control Cade twenty-four seven. He needs firm handling. No, don't come any closer," he barked at Quinn who had edged closer to them. "Cade is mine. You can't have him. He needs a real man."

The icy arrogance sent a cold chill through Cade. It was obvious nothing Quinn said had gotten through to Gareth. Did he really think Cade was just going to submit to him now? How self-absorbed was he?

"I'm not yours. I'll never be yours. You were my driver and I thought a friend, but I'm sorry, I don't feel that way about you. You really should leave now."

"The only place he's going is to a prison cell," Quinn said coldly.

"I don't think so." Gareth pointed a gun at Cade. "Come near me and I shoot him," he warned Quinn.

Cade stopped breathing. He had never come face-to-face with a gun. Never had much curiosity about them, his interests in art and music taking up all his time. Facing the muzzle of a gun was terrifying.

"You don't want to hurt Cade. You love him," Quinn said, all the while looking at Cade, his warm expression telling him everything would be all right.

"Yeah, but if I can't have him, you can't have him either."

"You don't need to hurt us," Cade said. "I'll come with you."

Gareth hauled him against him, his grip surprisingly

strong. Cade could smell his sweat, a sharp acrid smell that got to the back of Cade's throat, making him want to gag.

"Move," Gareth ordered, and he pointed the gun at Cade.

Cade kept his eyes on Quinn who gave the slightest of nods. Cade would obey his Daddy. Gareth pulled him out of the kitchen door to the house and into the back yard, slamming the door on Quinn and locking it.

"Where are you taking me?" Cade asked as Gareth hauled him across the yard. He'd expected to be forced into the car.

"None of your business," Gareth snapped.

They were three quarters of the way across the lawn that stretched the length of the back yard when Cade heard Quinn call out, but Gareth didn't slow down. Cade closed his eyes. Whatever happened to him, Quinn would not let him face it alone.

I love you, Quinn Ryder.

He hoped, if there was justice in the world, Quinn would hear that.

Yelling behind them made Gareth turn. Padraig, Doug, and Ronan bolted across the grass toward them. Taking advantage of the distraction, Quinn charged Gareth and Cade like a bull in a china shop. Gareth swung the gun around and fired. Even outside, the noise hurt Cade's ears. To his horror, Quinn grunted and staggered back a couple of steps, a red patch blooming at the top of his shoulder, but he kept going, sheer fury on his face.

"Keep away from me," Gareth yelled.

In the confusion, he let go of Cade who stumbled away, and Quinn dove into Gareth, the momentum sending them over the stone wall at the end of the yard. Cade screamed as they disappeared from view.

Chapter Fifteen

Quinn

Quinn twisted and managed to land on his feet, ignoring the screaming pain in his shoulder. Gareth was not so lucky, and landed with a snap of bone that made Quinn flinch. He cried out in agony and tumbled to the ground. Quinn was on him in an instant, pinning him into the dirt.

"My leg," Gareth groaned. "I broke my leg."

"Yeah," Quinn snapped. "You shot me. I don't give a shit." He looked up to see Doug and Padraig jumping over the edge, and Cade's anxious face. "Stay up there, Cade." Then to Doug, "You took your fucking time."

"We were locked in a garage," Doug groused. "Fucker jumped us with that gun. Where is it?"

"I've got it," Ronan said.

Cade jumped down and hauled Quinn into his arms. Quinn held back a yelp of pain, just thankful his beautiful boy was alive.

"Your shoulder. God, I'm sorry." Cade tried to let go but

Quinn held on just as tight to Cade, ignoring the melee around them.

"It's a graze, nothing more. I've been shot before."

Cade snorted against his chest. "If that's supposed to make me feel better, it's not working."

Quinn grinned above Cade's head. If his boy could be snarky, he was fine. That was all that mattered.

"Is he all right?" Cade asked after a while, as they watched Doug and Padraig work on Gareth.

"He'll live," Quinn said grimly.

Quinn's first aid skills were basic at best. He was ready, should the fucker try to escape. From the amount of noise Gareth made, he wasn't going anywhere.

I should have gutted him.

Eric, Tessie, and Gareth had all violated Cade in one form or another. He hoped Tessie would back off now she'd had a personal conversation with Cade. If not, she'd be receiving another visit from Dominic and/or a restraining order. Eric had done awful things to Cade before Long's machinations. But he was home free with no consequences. Somehow Quinn was going to make Eric pay for hurting his love.

EMTs arrived, and Doug and Padraig relinquished their places to the professionals.

One of the EMT's squinted at Quinn's blood-stained shirt. "Is that yours or his?"

Quinn shrugged and then wished he hadn't. "He shot me. It's just a graze. I'm fine."

"Let me take a look at it."

Quinn was about to refuse but he caught the storm brewing in Cade's eyes. He submitted to a bandage on the bullet wound, but the EMT agreed with his assessment that it was minor.

"You were lucky," the EMT said.

"He was a lousy shot."

Then Quinn saw the white-faced anguish on Cade's face. He thanked the EMT and put his arm around Cade to draw him away. "This isn't your fault, boy. You need to stop blaming yourself."

"How is it not my fault?" Cade demanded. "If it hadn't been for me, you wouldn't have been shot."

"Bodyguard, love. It goes with the territory."

From the fierce scowl Cade gave him, that was the wrong thing to say too.

Padraig joined them, wearing a strangely satisfied expression.

"Why're you looking so smug?" Quinn asked.

"I found out who sent the note," Padraig said.

"Long?"

Padraig shook his head. "Ronan." He laughed at Quinn's stunned expression. "Don't worry. He's not another stalker. Long dropped it. He'd been planning to send Cade a series of notes. We found them in the garage. Ronan recognized the style and said he'd picked up one by the gates and given it to the delivery guy, thinking he was the one who dropped it."

Finally, they had the last piece of the puzzle.

"Why did Gareth think I'd fallen in love with him?" Cade murmured.

Quinn held Cade close to him. "Who knows? Maybe he was lonely and that turned friendship into something more sinister?"

"That's a very generous motive," Doug said. "Maybe he was just your average psycho."

Cade shivered. Quinn was relieved at the approach of two police officers. There were a lot of questions to answer. Quinn had to explain how he ended up getting shot and then falling over the wall with Gareth.

As Gareth was wheeled away, still moaning, the older grizzled cop side-eyed Cade. "You're Cade Connolly."

"Yes, sir," Cade said, burrowing close to Quinn.

The cop raised his eyebrow at Quinn. "And you are?"

"His boyfriend," Quinn said curtly. "Quinn Ryder."

"And you work for CDR."

"I do."

"And this man," the officer paused as he checked his notebook, "was your driver, Gareth Long?"

"He was, as well as working for my record company," Cade agreed. "He lives above the garage."

"But you discovered he was stalking you."

"Yes," Quinn said.

"When did you discover this?"

"Today," Cade sighed. "We had no idea he was hiding out in the house and watching us. I've no idea how long he's been in the attic."

"Creepy fucker," Padraig muttered.

The cop hummed. "And you've had other issues?"

"If by issues you mean a jealous ex who couldn't let go and a fan who stalked me wherever I went, then yes."

"You're very popular, Mr. Connolly," the officer said dryly.

Cade leaned back, seeking Quinn's support. Quinn held him close, refusing to let him go even for a moment. "All the crazies love me right now."

"And what is CDR doing here?"

"You know us?" Quinn asked.

"Yes." It didn't sound complimentary.

"Cade's management called us in a week ago to help

with an issue. What we didn't realize was that Cade was facing more than one hostile."

"A middle-aged woman and a driver are hardly hostiles," the cop suggested.

"It depends if you're on the end of their gun," Quinn snapped.

The officer nodded, as if Quinn had a point. "We need you to come down to the precinct to give a statement."

Quinn opened his mouth to object, but Cade got there first. "Officer, could we do it here or at CDR? I really would prefer to keep the publicity as low as possible." He gave a wry smile. "Between my ex, the fan, and now my driver, I think I've given the media enough gossip material."

"I'd have thought this would be good publicity."

Cade shook his head. "Not this time. I just want to get through the event this weekend as smoothly as possible."

"We can do it here. Long admitted to spying on you."

Quinn raised his eyebrow. "He did?"

"Oh yeah. While he was begging for pain relief. It's amazing what you'll confess to, when you're in agony. I don't think you'll have to worry about him returning anytime soon. He'll be in traction for weeks."

Cade winced but Quinn felt no remorse at taking Gareth over the wall. His only aim had been to get him away from Cade, and he'd succeeded.

"Let's go back to the house," Quinn suggested. "We're only in the way here."

"Stay away from the attic," the cop ordered.

Quinn had no intention of taking Cade anywhere near the attic. He'd be happy to have the whole thing sealed off. Maybe Cade would consider moving.

They linked fingers and wandered slowly in the direction of the house. Quinn was exhausted, his shoulder really ached, and he wasn't paying attention when Cade suddenly stopped.

"Look!" He pointed at the house.

"What?" Quinn squinted in the direction of his finger.

"I couldn't work out how Gareth got in the attic. But you can see. The windows are open between his apartment and the gable window. It's a narrow gap."

Quinn nodded. "It would have been so easy to slide over."

"He's been spying on me for a long time, hasn't he?"

"I don't know, boy. But it's over now. He's gone. He's not coming back."

Ever!

Quinn admitted he had a lot of Neanderthal in him, but Gareth Long wouldn't get within a hundred miles of Cade Connolly again.

"I can't help feeling sorry for him," Cade said, as he wrapped his arms around himself. "I didn't know he felt like that about me."

Quinn pulled Cade against him and held him so close, Cade protested he couldn't breathe. "You have a big heart, but you can't be expected to know your employees have the hots for you." There was a long silence for a moment and Cade's shoulders shook. "Don't cry, love." Cade's shoulders shook even harder. Quinn groaned when he suddenly realized Cade was laughing. "Cade!"

Cade raised his head and tears were running down his cheeks, but he was definitely laughing. "I'm sorry, but you've got to admit that it's funny."

"I'm not your employee."

"You are, though."

"Maybe, but I'm nothing like him," Quinn insisted.

"No, you're not," Cade purred. "*Nothing* like him."

Quinn was somewhat mollified. Then he caught the gleam in Cade's eyes. "Nothing like him," he agreed.

Cade stood on tiptoe and whispered a suggestion in his ear.

Quinn pressed his rock-hard dick into Cade's belly. "You're very feisty, boy, but I can do that."

Cade pulled back with a frown. "Am I too much?"

"No, don't ever think that." Quinn grabbed his hands and put them against his heart. "If you want something, you ask for it. I might not always agree, but you can always ask. I'd love the idea of bathing you when the cops are gone."

"How did I get so lucky to find you?"

Quinn asked himself that every day. "Right backatcha, little boy." He looked over his shoulder and saw the cops were still busy. "Why don't we go back for a drink and we can snuggle until the police want to talk to us?"

"I like that idea," Cade agreed and held his hand all the way back to the house.

Cade

After the cops left, Quinn had bathed Cade slowly and luxuriously and brought him to a climax that turned him inside out, then showered himself and changed into loose-fitting shorts and a tank top. The bandage was a stark white contrast to his tanned skin and ink, but Cade had almost gotten to the point where he could look at it without feeling guilty. Almost.

Quinn fell asleep on the couch in the den while Cade curled up in the chair opposite, Mogs on his lap, idly doodling on a pad. Cade found the silence almost oppressive, now they were alone in the house.

Alone. Cade shuddered. How many times had he

thought he was alone, only to have Gareth watch him? How had he never realized Gareth was obsessed with him? Cade thought about their relationship, but he still couldn't see it. He thought back to a conversation he'd had with Quinn the previous night. They'd been watching a movie when a thought had occurred to him.

"Doug said he was surprised you agreed to take this case," Cade had said. "He said you didn't work for CDR now."

"I take odd cases but I don't work just for them," Quinn said.

Cade had noticed the tightness in his voice. "What happened?" When Quinn didn't reply he said, "It's okay, Daddy, you don't have to tell me."

Quinn had smiled sadly and ran his fingers through Cade's hair. "I can't think of anyone else I'd rather tell than my boy. Friends of mine got involved in a case a few years ago. I found out one of them, a man I called my brother, was an addict and a murderer. I loved that man and I had no idea what he'd done. Nor did any of us, including his twin brother. I couldn't believe my judgement of people was that poor. I needed time away from CDR to think. It just ended up being more time than I expected."

Cade had wrapped his arms around Quinn and encouraged him to lay his head against Cade's chest. Quinn resisted for a moment, but then he'd rolled over and accepted Cade's comfort.

Now Cade knew what Quinn meant. How could you see something when you weren't looking for it? Gareth had been obsessed, yet in their interactions he'd been the same friendly guy Cade had always known. How far would he have gone?

Cade shuddered again and searched for something else

to think about. He grinned as Quinn snorted, smacked his lips and wriggled to find a more comfortable position. He didn't look younger, but unguarded, without the mantle of authority he wore during the day. Cade noticed Quinn's flaccid cock poking out from the leg of his rucked-up shorts. Would his Daddy mind if he drew him like this? He watched Quinn sleeping for a moment, then he picked up his pad and pencils. He would show Quinn when he woke, but for now this moment was just his, just like Quinn.

* * *

Quinn studied the pencil sketch of him while Cade waited, unable to breathe.

"You're so talented," Quinn said, awe clear in his voice.

"You don't mind that I didn't ask first?" Cade had to be sure.

Quinn cupped Cade's neck and drew him in for a kiss. "Mind that the world-famous artist, ConC, drew me? I'm honored, my boy."

"But you were asleep and vulnerable."

"Cade, you can draw me any time. Consent is given."

"Even naked?"

Quinn waggled his eyebrows. "Especially naked."

"I love drawing nude men," Cade admitted. "I don't get much chance now."

"You can draw me. We'll have to discuss you drawing other men."

"Eric didn't want me seeing nude men."

Quinn shrugged. "If you discuss it with me, I'm okay with it. Some of the Daddies might like to be drawn with their boys."

Excitement wriggled through Cade. "Really? I'd love to

draw couples together, clothed or unclothed. Can you arrange that?"

"I'll talk to the men I know. They don't get much opportunity to be open with their boys. They'll probably leap at the chance."

"I'd like to draw Ian and his Daddy," Cade said. "I owe him an apology for the way I treated him."

Quinn's chuckle was like the low rumble of their Hogs. "Ian's a kind-hearted boy. He won't hold it against you, but I'll talk to Graham. I've got to ask though, I thought you were a street artist."

"I am," Cade agreed. "I love the freedom of street art, but I don't just use one medium. I also sculpt."

The awe was back in Quinn's face. "Is there anything you can't do?"

"I can't cook," Cade pointed out.

"You draw, I'll cook, and maybe we can teach each other something."

Cade smiled at him. "I'd love that." Then he swallowed as Quinn's smile turned predatory. "Daddy?"

Quinn stood and stretched, wincing a little, his shorts slipping to graze the thick curls at the base of his cock. Cade licked his lips as he gazed at Quinn's exposed furry belly.

Quinn held out his hand. "Now, I think we need to do something else."

"Like what?" Cade said without thinking, as he put his hand in Quinn's. His Daddy had exposed him to so many wonderful things.

"I need to claim you without any psycho trying to take you as his," Quinn said. "Or hers."

"I hope it's all over," Cade said anxiously.

"If it isn't, we'll find them too," Quinn said, with a grim expression. Then he smiled at Cade and the grimness eased.

"But for now it's just you and me in here. I'm going to lay you on the couch and make love to you for hours."

"You could just fuck me." Cade gave him a cheeky grin. He wasn't fussy as long as he had Quinn's thick cock from balls to tip inside him, but Quinn shook his head, a frown on his face as if he didn't like being contradicted.

"No."

Realizing he'd screwed up, Cade said, "I'm sorry, Daddy."

Quinn's frown was replaced by a warm smile. "It's all right, boy. Sometimes I like fucking you, but sometimes I want to make love slow and gentle."

"Show me?" Cade begged.

And Quinn did, with exquisite gentleness that made Cade want to weep.

* * *

The run up to the bike event seemed to be an endless round of interviews with the media, interviews with the police, rehearsals with the band, Quinn throwing food down Cade's throat whether he liked it or not, and one blissful ride into the mountains with the Hogs. Cade's head was spinning. But he had Quinn at his back and his Daddy cum boyfriend cum bodyguard intervened every time he felt Cade got overwhelmed, or when Cade looked at him in desperation.

But the day of the event had finally arrived, and Cade couldn't wait for it to happen and to be all over.

Louis Romero met them behind the stage, greeting them with a huge smile. Cade had known him since the band formed. Louis owned an event management company and was handling the entertainment for the show, with

Daysance headlining the bill. He was a well-muscled, tall, Latino man with the gentlest smile Cade had ever seen. And a boy. Cade had to process what he knew about this man as a business shark and a boy. Maybe he'd ask if they could talk when he came back from London.

Romero saw Quinn and his smile broadened with that same joy Ian had worn. "Quinn, good to see you. It's been too long." He held out his hand and Quinn shook it.

Cade felt anger rise up inside him. God, had Quinn fucked every boy in Seattle? Then Quinn laid a hand against his lower back and Cade felt the anger drain away. He swore he heard the silent order. "Calm, boy."

"I'm so pleased you two met," Louis said to Cade.

Cade blinked. "You are?"

"Quinn was waiting a long time for the right... guy."

"Enough, Louis," Quinn said firmly.

Louis's lips twitched but he nodded.

Cade felt more relaxed. "Maybe we could talk when I get back from London?"

"Love to," Louis said. "I've got to go. See you at the party after the show."

Cade leaned into Quinn as Louis strode away with a coterie of men after him. "Why does he look so sad when he's not smiling?"

Quinn sighed. "Because he met the Daddy of his dreams, and it didn't work out."

"Poor man."

Cade was so fucking lucky.

Now as Cade waited for his cue, he felt the buzz through his bones as he always did before a gig. This was his moment. He was ready to make the crowd roar, loud and long. He looked around and Quinn was five feet behind him, close enough if Cade needed him but not close enough to disturb him as he focused on what he was about to do.

"You'll be here when I come off?" Cade asked.

"I'll be here for you," Quinn promised.

No Daddy, no boy. That was all for later in private.

"Get a room, you two," Keith groused as he joined them.

"You're just jealous cos my man can cook," Cade teased.

"I'm just jealous cos you found yourself a hot daddy... and he can cook."

They all stared at him, including Dave and Ian.

He rolled his eyes. "I'm not as stupid as I look, assholes." He flipped them all off as they hooted at him.

"You don't mind?" Cade asked tentatively.

"What the fuck do I care?" Keith said. "As long as you're not inviting me into your bed, we're fine."

Then Cade started laughing because Quinn gagged behind him.

Keith flipped them off, which made Cade laugh even harder.

"Daysance, you're up!"

Cade rushed back, kissed Quinn and looked up at him. "Thank you for getting me here, Daddy. I love you."

He said it low, but he needed Quinn to hear.

Quinn gave him that lazy, sexy smile. "Just wait until afterward, my boy. I love you so much."

Cade couldn't wait. He strode toward the front of the stage, fists pumping the air. Now he had to be Cade Connolly. But later he'd be Quinn's boy and his Daddy would cuddle him on his lap and remind him of the only thing that mattered.

Them.

Epilogue

Quinn

Quinn paced through the foyer of Cade's house. Ten steps forward, fourteen steps across, ten steps back. And so on. He'd been pacing since he'd gotten the call that Cade had landed. Cade had begged him to wait at the house, as he wanted their meeting to be private. Quinn had growled at him, but he'd agreed, on the understanding Cade came straight to the house. He needed to know his boy was all right.

The past two months had seemed like an eternity. Quinn had been set to go with Cade when a high-profile case involving Louis Romero arose at CDR, and they needed Quinn. He'd refused, but Dominic had virtually gotten on his knees to beg him to take the case. To his surprise, Cade agreed with Dominic. Quinn had been hurt until Cade took him in his arms and pointed out that there was a boy who needed Quinn, and he couldn't turn his back on them. Quinn had reluctantly agreed on one condition. He called Liam Quick and pointed out that if one hair was harmed on his boy's head, he would come over to London and eviscerate Quick.

"You can try," Quick had said.

"Sure of yourself, are you?"

"Your boy is safe. Nothing will happen to him," Quick had said, and Quinn was sure he could hear Quick rolling his eyes over the long-distance call.

Ten steps forward, fourteen steps across, ten steps back.

He heard the sound of a car engine and flung open the door to find Cade getting out. Quinn didn't see anyone else. He didn't care. Fuck private, he couldn't wait any longer. Quinn bolted down the steps to haul Cade into his arms and pick him up. Cade wrapped his arms around Quinn's neck and his legs around Quinn's waist, babbling in his ear. The only word Quinn could make out was 'Daddy.' He ground his mouth on Cade's and they kissed hot and wet, not caring that they had an audience.

"Jeez, you couldn't have waited five minutes," Keith groused.

Quinn flipped him off, not breaking the kiss, then he carried Cade into the house and slammed the door.

"My luggage, Daddy," Cade murmured against his lips.

"Can wait outside," Quinn growled and stalked upstairs with Cade still in his arms, ignoring Mogs's attempt to greet Cade.

He took Cade into his bedroom and set him gently down on his feet, shutting the door on Mogs's protest. He looked down at his boy, noting the lines of fatigue and worry in his eyes. Despite Quinn's kissing Cade, his boy was obviously still unsure of his welcome.

Cade stared up at him with such naked want that Quinn's body went on full arousal.

"I can't believe I'm back home with you," he murmured. "It feels like an eternity."

"It was an eternity," Quinn declared.

Cade curled his fingers into Quinn's knit sweater. "I was wrong, Daddy."

"You were?"

"I wanted to show you I could cope without you. That I was strong enough to let you do your work, and I'd do mine."

"Nothing is more important than you," Quinn declared. "Nothing. I should have been there for you."

"I needed you so badly," Cade admitted.

"You should have called me, boy. I'd have been on the first plane to London."

Cade's eyes darkened at 'boy' as Quinn knew it would. "You were busy and then I was busy."

"I would have come."

"I know."

They'd barely spoken to each other because of the time zones and their work. Communication had been reduced to messages and rare phone calls.

"I'm not doing that again," Quinn said. "Next time, I go with you."

"But your job."

"I resigned from CDR last week. Properly this time. There's no going back."

This wasn't true. Dominic would have him back in an instant if he called, but Quinn wasn't leaving Cade's side again.

"You did?" A myriad of emotions passed over Cade's beautiful face: joy, relief, concern and, Quinn was sure, a little fear.

"I'm not going anywhere," Quinn promised, holding Cade closer.

"You're staying with me?"

"I will be sticking to your side like glue. I'm your new head of security."

Cade leaned back in his arms, his eyes comically wide and his mouth pursed into an O. "You are, but how?"

Quinn sighed. "Do you want to talk about it now or can I strip you naked, throw you on the bed, and fuck you through the mattress first?"

Cade pretended to think for half a second before he hauled off his jacket and kicked off his shoes. Quinn stripped off his own sweater, then slipped his hands under Cade's long-sleeved T-shirt and hauled it over his head. Cade hissed as Quinn's knuckles grazed his soft skin.

Quinn was so hard he felt like his dick was ready to drill through his jeans. It was obvious Cade felt the same, from the bulge in his pants. Quinn sank to his knees and unfastened them. He pulled the zipper down slowly, looking up to see Cade's reaction. Cade's attention was solely focused on Quinn's hands. Quinn could swear he wasn't breathing.

"Boy," he rumbled.

Cade looked into Quinn's eyes. "Yes?"

"I love you."

Cade's eyes softened. "I love you so much, my Daddy."

"Remember, whether I'm with you or not, I still love you."

"You don't think I'm weak for not wanting to leave you?" Cade sounded so unsure of himself.

"I've never thought you were weak," Quinn said. "You're a very strong man, Cade."

He expected Cade to protest, but Cade seemed to draw strength from the words. "Touch me," Cade begged.

Quinn tugged Cade's pants and briefs over his slim hips and down his thighs. His slender cock bounced against his belly. "You've kept yourself smooth for me."

"I shaved last night," Cade confessed. "It wasn't so easy to shave myself."

Quinn smiled, pressing his face into Cade's groin, feeling a couple of raspy spots where Cade had missed. He would make his boy smooth tomorrow. Now was for reconnecting. He inhaled his musky scent, having missed this so much. Then he kissed around the base of Cade's cock.

"If you want to fuck me, you'd better get on with it," Cade gasped. "I'm not sure I can wait."

"You'll wait as long as I want, boy. You're not coming until I let you, or there will be consequences." Quinn grinned, loving Cade's shudder. "Have you touched yourself?" Quinn added the growl to his voice that he knew Cade loved.

"A couple of times." Quinn had given Cade permission to masturbate while they were separated. "I wasn't really interested, to be honest. I used up my energy on stage."

Now his cock was very interested, leaving a sticky trail on his belly.

Quinn licked up the pre-come, swirling his tongue around the glans.

"Fuck me now!" Cade somehow managed to make that a plea rather than an order.

Quinn sucked hard once on his cock, drawing a long groan from Cade. Then he got to his feet, picked Cade up, and laid him on the bed as if he were the most precious creature in the world, which he was. He stripped off the rest of Cade's clothing and focused on his own. Cade never took his eyes off Quinn for a second. Then he climbed on and settled between Cade's legs. Cade drew his legs up, exposing his hole, his vulnerability a gift. Quinn bent forward and brushed his lips over Cade's balls.

"Quinn," Cade whined.

Quinn smiled. He reached for the condom and lube. Both of them wanted to go bare, but they'd agreed to wait until they got tested on Cade's return. Quinn would never take a chance with Cade's health. He'd booked appointments for the following day. He'd never take a chance, but he wasn't going to wait a second longer than he had to.

A snick of the cap and cool slick pooled into his palm. He warmed it between his fingers and rimmed the delicate ring of muscle. Cade's happy sigh when Quinn slid into him made the pain of separation feel a million miles away. He took his time to prepare Cade, as it had been many weeks, until Cade begged him to hurry the hell up. Not so much pleading that time. Then Cade apologized and asked him very nicely to hurry the hell up.

Quinn could have strung it out, but it wasn't like he didn't want to be inside his boy. He placed Cade's legs over his shoulders and sank into the warm, welcoming heat.

"Now I am home," Cade gasped.

Quinn leaned forward to brush Cade's lips, making Cade cry out. "Welcome home, my boy. Never leave me again."

"Never," Cade promised. "I'm never leaving my Daddy."

Promise asked and given, Quinn made love to Cade until his boy was a sated pool of desire.

Cade

Cade didn't want to move from the bed, even as sweat cooled on his skin and made him shiver. Quinn gathered him closer against his warm body.

"I dreamed about this," Cade said, tilting his head to stare into Quinn's liquid chocolate eyes.

"Making love?"

"Being in bed with you. You holding me. I didn't feel safe until you held me close again."

Quinn bent to kiss him. Cade turned in his arms to face Quinn, and for long moments he didn't think about anything else except Quinn's mouth on his.

When they pulled away from each other to breathe, Quinn said, "I want to show you something."

"Okay." He noticed Quinn seemed nervous. "Is something wrong?"

"No." Quinn smiled at him. "I did a little rearranging while you were away."

Cade nodded. "I know. We talked about it. You said you wanted to bring your gym equipment here."

Quinn kissed Cade's bare shoulder. "Come with me."

Cade recognized it as an order, and although he'd rather have spent more time cuddling in bed with his Daddy, he stood and took Quinn's hand. "Where are we going?"

"I put the gym equipment in the bedroom I had. It can easily be pushed aside if we have guests."

Cade liked the sound of 'we have guests.'

Quinn led him down the hall to the end bedroom which they'd agreed would be the gym. It had originally been the nursery for the previous occupant. He stood outside the closed door and gazed down at Cade.

"In my apartment I had a room like this which I used for

my boys."

Cade frowned and Quinn shook his head. "Everything in here is new. I'm not expecting you to use anything that was used by another boy."

"What is it? Whips and chains?" Cade teased. "St. Andrew's cross?"

"Not exactly."

Quinn opened the door and stood back to let Cade precede him into the room. Cade's mouth went dry.

It was painted in sky blue, a contrast to the pale pink before. But whereas before it had been full of storage boxes Cade had never unpacked, now there was a table with pads of paper and pens and crayons by the window. A low bed on the other side just right for a nap. There were dinosaurs on the covers. Crates filled with toys were placed against one wall. The room didn't look complete. More like it was waiting for someone to fill it.

Cade turned to him. "It's—"

"It's a playroom," Quinn said.

"For—"

"For littles."

"But I'm not a little," Cade protested.

Quinn stroked down one cheek. "Are you sure about that?"

Cade opened his mouth to deny he was a little, but the words seemed to stick in his throat.

"It's not shameful, boy. It's a sign of strength to acknowledge that side of yourself."

Cade shook his head. "I can't be a little."

Quinn wrapped his arms around Cade and encouraged him to rest his head on Quinn's chest. "The first boy I met didn't know he was a little either, but there were clues."

"Like?"

"He loved to draw and color."

"So do a lot of people."

"He loved playing with kids' toys. He had shelves of toys never taken out of their boxes."

"Perhaps he collected them," Cade's voice was harsh.

Quinn stroked his head. "He sucked his thumb."

Cade stiffened. "How did you know?"

"I watch you when you're asleep," Quinn said. "He was a CEO and always stressed. He'd been told if he didn't reduce his stress levels, he'd have a heart attack. I encouraged him to play with some of the toys and color. It went from there."

"Do you still see him?"

"No. He found a Daddy of his own."

"I'm sorry." Cade ached at how many boys Quinn had lost to other Daddies.

"I'm not. Gianno was half his age and three times as dominant as me. It was a match made in heaven." Quinn pressed a kiss on top of his head. "Why don't you get dressed? There are clothes in the chest. I'll make us a drink and a snack and come back here." He kissed Cade and left him standing in the middle of the room.

"What the hell?" Cade said out loud.

He felt odd being naked in here. He opened up the chest and found T-shirts, shorts, and briefs. It didn't escape his notice that they had a childish quality to them. He picked up the top blue T-shirt. It had a rocket on it. For a moment he contemplated returning to his bedroom to get pajama pants and a hoody, but then he stroked the soft cotton of the T-shirt. He shrugged it on and found briefs with rockets, too. He smiled as he stepped into them. By the time he was dressed, Cade was starting to feel better.

He wandered over to the table by the window and

looked down at the pad of paper. Quinn had written *'Cade's pad,'* on it in his messy scrawl. Just the thoughtfulness made his eyes sting. Cade tried hard not to think about Eric, but he couldn't help comparing him to Quinn. Eric would never have thought of doing this, just on a few clues.

He'd gotten a call while he was in London from Leo, apologizing for not seeing the damage Eric did to him and the other boys. Cade had offered to contribute to legal fees, but Leo assured him the community could handle it. A warrant was out for Eric's arrest on charges of sexual assault, but he had vanished. No one had seen him for weeks.

Cade sat in a chair and picked a brown pencil which reminded him of Quinn's eyes. By the time Quinn returned with a tray, Cade was engrossed in his sketch.

"You look busy," Quinn said. He'd taken time to dress in his plaid pajama pants and a long-sleeved T-shirt. He carefully put the tray on a small table by the armchair and looked over Cade's shoulder. "Is that me?"

"It is." Cade looked up. "Do you mind?"

"Of course not. I told you it's fine. I love it, boy. Do I really look that scowly?"

"I thought of you shouting at Eric."

"Ah. I understand." Quinn gently patted Cade's back, careful not to knock him. "Would you like a drink?"

Cade looked at the tray, expecting to see coffee. Instead there were two sandwiches cut into smaller pieces, chips, a bowl filled with chopped fruit, and one cup of coffee. The other cup was a kid's cup filled with milk.

"Is that for me?"

Quinn nodded. "I'd like you to sit on my lap." He pointed to the comfy-looking armchair.

"Why?"

"Because I like to feed my littles."

"You want to feed me?" Cade had a sudden memory of Quinn feeding him with omelet.

Quinn nodded and sat in the chair. He patted his thighs. "You've sat on my lap before."

He had, but now it had a whole different meaning. Quinn just waited, not trying to coerce him into making a decision. Cade bit his lip. He liked sitting on Quinn's lap and Quinn had fed him before. Okay, that had been strawberries and chocolate sauce and had led to an intense night of fucking, where Cade had cuffed Quinn's hands to the bedframe and ridden his cock until he'd forgotten his own name, but it wasn't like it would be new. He got up and stumbled over to Quinn, who patted his lap again. Cade settled against Quinn and let Quinn hold him for a moment.

"Good boy," Quinn murmured.

Cade's tummy growled and Quinn chuckled. "I think I need to feed the hungry dragon."

"Dinosaur, Daddy. It's a dinosaur, not a dragon. Dragons are for big people."

He waited for Quinn to contradict him, but Quinn just nodded. "Of course it's a dinosaur." Quinn picked up one of the sandwich pieces. "Here's a sandwich for the hungry dinosaur." He waved it around and popped it into Cade's open mouth. Cade hastily chewed as Quinn looked at him expectantly. Then Quinn repeated the exercise. As he handed him the sippy cup, Cade wasn't sure what to make of it. It was bizarre. But by the time they'd gotten through the cheese sandwich and the chips, and the fruit because Quinn insisted, Cade was feeling more relaxed than he could ever remember. It had been fun, a little silly, but right too.

"I don't know if anyone ever did this with me," he murmured as he rested in Quinn's lap after the snack. He couldn't remember any of his foster parents playing with him, although he'd blocked a lot of the memories from that time.

"We can do this whenever you need it," Quinn suggested.

"And whenever you need it too," Cade insisted.

"Yes, when I need it too. I get a lot of pleasure from taking care of you."

Cade chewed on his bottom lip and then summoned up his courage to ask, "Will you still take care of other boys?"

Quinn kissed the top of his head. "No. I'm only your Daddy. And you are my only boy."

Cade sighed in relief and leaned against Quinn's chest. He was feeling sleepy again, jetlag catching up with him. "How did Dominic take your resignation?"

"He's not happy." Quinn's tone suggested he didn't care much one way or the other.

"Are you sure?"

"We'll talk about it later, boy. In here, it's Daddy and his little. No grownup stuff."

Cade thought about that for a while. "I like that."

They sat in silence, Quinn holding him close. Cade sucked his thumb a little and Quinn said nothing.

"Will I have to wear diapers?" he asked after a while.

"Only if you want to," Quinn said. "Nothing happens in here that you don't want."

"I never thought I could have this," Cade murmured.

"What? Diapers?"

Cade grinned, but he answered honestly. "Happiness."

Quinn held him tight. "I promise I will try to make you happy every day."

"Even when I'm being a brat?" Because, being a brat, Cade had to poke the tiger.

"Especially when you're being a brat, because you'll know that I still love you."

"You do? Really love me?" God, when was he going to learn to trust?

"Bones to balls, my boy," Quinn said. "I love you, bones to balls."

THE END

Hurry on over to read Louis's story in ***Hold Close***.
"I'll get down on my knees if I have to, Daddy."

Louis knows only one bodyguard he can trust to take care of him after a vicious assault. He's prepared go to his knees and beg his former Daddy to help him. But will Craig listen?

After his relationship with Louis ended, Craig ran away so he'd never have to face his boy again. But when Louis pleads for his help, Craig has a tough decision to make; risk his heart being broken for a second time or turn away from the man who needs him.

In Craig's head, Louis is a client in danger. In his heart, Louis is his boy. In his hands, Louis is his world. Will Louis and Craig grasp their second chance in love, or will they walk away from each other at the end of the assignment?

If you like a passionate second chance romance and reverse age gap daddy/boy relationship, ***Hold Close*** *is for you.*

* * *

Want more Quinn and Cade?
Join my newsletter to read about Quinn facing himself
naked in an art gallery.

* * *

Dominic, Josh and CDR are introduced in my enemies-to-lovers adventure series. ***Angel Securities***...who is Charlie and why does he know a lot more about Josh than Josh does about him?

Also by Sue Brown

Love Sue's work? Support her at **Ream**. You'll get exclusive content and access to new books before anyone else.

You can find all of Sue's books over at **her website**. Don't forget to sign up for her newsletter **here**.

About Sue Brown

Sue Brown is a Londoner with a dream to live on a small island. Coffee fuels her addiction to writing romance with hot guys loving each other, and her Adorkadog snores in harmony as she creates.

Come over and talk to Sue at:
Sue's Subscribe: https://reamstories.com/suebrownstories
Newsletter: http://bit.ly/SueBrownNews
Bookbub: https://www.bookbub.com/profile/sue-brown
TikTok: https://www.tiktok.com/@suebrownstories
Her website: http://www.suebrownstories.com/
Author group – Facebook: https://www.facebook.com/groups/suebrownstories/
Facebook: https://www.facebook.com/SueBrownsStories/
Email: sue@suebrownstories.com